JOURNEY INTO THE PAST

ABE F. MARCH

Contributing author: Lynn Jett

ISBN 13: 978-0-9822722-8-2
ISBN: 0-9822722-86
Library of Congress Control Number: 2009925459

"Du, Du Liegst Mir Im Herzen" reprinted
with permission of Thomas Keyes

Cover design by All Things That Matter Press
Cover photos courtesy of Abe F. March
Published in 2009 by All Things That Matter Press
Printed in the United States of America

Young, attractive, and successful, Heather Wilson is a force to be reckoned with. A star on the rise in one of the most powerful architectural firms in the country, she appears to have it all – that is, until she walks in on her husband of 18 years in the heat of passion with another woman. In the ensuing emotional fallout, she tries to bury herself in work, but when she happens across a photo of an ancient German castle one day, she is instantly drawn to it – and the older gentleman staring back at her from within it – for reasons she can't fully explain, and she soon embarks on a journey to the site in order to explore her feelings further.

Upon her arrival, she meets Hans, the gentleman from the photo, and the two of them form a connection that soon evolves into all-out attraction – the only problem: he's a married man, and his wife has been in a coma for five years; nonetheless, Hans can't deny the intensity of the bond between him and Heather, and, despite his loyalty to his beloved, he can't resist indulging in the burgeoning passion that soon consumes them both. What neither Heather nor Hans realize, though, is that the attraction they feel for one another has deep spiritual roots and has endured for centuries – and the ultimate outcome of their not-so-random encounter lies just beyond the scope of their control…

Journey Into The Past is a touching tale of the incomparable power of fate. In it, author Abe March takes the reader on a compelling journey through the mysterious inner workings of the heart, putting on full display just how mercurial the world of emotions can often be. He also treats the reader to a revealing trek through the culture, countryside, and fascinating history of Germany, lending his narrative a healthy dose of genuine authenticity.

Love comes in many different forms, some of which often take us completely by surprise. In **Journey Into The Past**,

though, Abe March does a skillful job of proving that, no matter which form it ultimately takes, true love transcends all boundaries – even those of space and time.
-**Linda Waterson**, Apex Reviews

As simple and direct as Hemingway, March's narrative fashions a tale of love and power overshadowed by the ill-intents of others. The messages conveyed in *Journey into the Past* are not only timely, but also universal in scope. Tantalizing and pushing metaphors to the edge of risqué, *Journey into the Past* will keep you warm and interested.
- **Brian L. Doe**, Author of *The Grace Note, Barley and Gold*, Co-Author of the *Waking God* series.

PROLOGUE

The orange tinge of scattered clouds encircled the castle like a halo. The castle was mostly a ruin, but the silhouette of this once majestic structure possessed an eerie sense of foreboding. The deep crevices and shadows held mysteries longing to be told. A lone hawk circled overhead in the quiet of dusk and suddenly dove after its prey. A loud shriek was heard by the victim of this attack before succumbing to a quick death.

Ivan awoke with a start. The recurring dream of the castle lying in ruins was something he could not discuss with anyone. He brushed it aside and prepared for the day. He knew he could never lay claim to the title of nobility, even though his father was a nobleman. He was simply a bastard. It made him angry that his mother had to suffer the humiliation of bearing a son by her lord. When the time was right, he would have to try to force his father to acknowledge him if he could ever hope to marry the girl he loved. Just now, he was simply a farmer whose owner was a nobleman. He would have to work the fields for several more years before he could have his own plot. He knew that his athletic prowess gave him much recognition, and it was at one of the games that he had first seen Lucile. The attraction happened the moment their eyes met. After that, Lucile attended every game in which he participated, and eventually he had the courage as well as the opportunity to speak with her. It was not easy since she was always in the company of guardians for young maidens with rank of nobility. They both sought an opportunity to meet, and it eventually happened.

It was now early in the 16th century, and laws regarding ownership and inheritance in many regions and cities were becoming explosive. Many cities all over Germany were experiencing civil unrest. Peasants had taken up arms and things were different. Yes, the peasants were poorly armed and inexperienced, but they posed a serious challenge. They assembled in Hordes and forced local knights to lead them. Initially they were able to inflict damage by burning down a few castles, but they were no match for disciplined armies of noble cavalier. The peasants' war came to an end. It was 1525; the Hordes were dispersed, and the ringleaders publicly executed.

Times were difficult. The love between Lucile and Ivan had many obstacles, yet Lucile devised a plan to be with her beloved Ivan.

Their forbidden love would ultimately take 20th century characters on a Journey into the Past.

CHAPTER ONE
THE GOOD WITH THE BAD

"What do you mean? How did the caterer lose the order?" Heather Wilson asked while twisting a strand of curly red hair around her finger. She stood staring out at the San Francisco skyline. "Yes, I'll wait while you check. This is only the biggest groundbreaking ceremony in this firm's history. We have to serve food!"

She paced the floor. She had long since kicked off her two-inch navy-blue pumps, worn to make a point when she needed to be taller than most of the men in the firm. Her pinstriped business suit, like her long curly red hair, seemed to have a mind of its own. One sleeve up, the other down; shirt tucked in on one side and not the other. The tailored skirt appeared to be two sizes too big and hung low on her hips. Half of her hair was tied back and the rest hung free. She was a wreck, and she knew it; she hadn't gone home last night or the night before. She'd stayed up working all night, and she hadn't slept but a few hours for three days. She whispered to herself, "Just one more day. One more day."

The voice came over the phone, "We found the order. That temporary receptionist put it under her name, not Kranshaw, Martin, and Wilson. The food will be delivered at eleven a.m. tomorrow, and served at noon, after the ground-breaking ceremony."

Heather collapsed into the leather chair and said, "Thanks so much, Karen. You are the greatest."

Heather placed the cordless phone in the recharge socket. She turned her chair and sat staring at the San Francisco skyline. It was this view, the buildings that created this silhouette against an orange red sunset, this skyline that had beckoned her to be an architect, and this same chair where her dad had sat. She was supposed to be creating great works of art and function, not chasing down catering orders. But as her dad had said, "It all comes with the territory. You've got to take the good with the bad."

The good would be watching the mayor cut the ribbon to her designed vision created out of stone, glass, and steel. The bad was chasing down catering orders. The good was watching her vision grow day by day; the bad was working endless late nights on last minute changes. The good was heading up a team of talented engineers and scientists feeding off each others' ideas; the bad was walking in on her husband of eighteen years feeding off the ample breast of another woman. Yeah, that was the really bad part of this project. He claimed she spent too much time away from home. She knew she just happened to show up at home at the wrong time.

She turned, facing her desk, and saw the round trip tickets to Tahiti on the corner. The senior partners had said, "Heather, if you bring this one in on time and on budget, there's three months off with pay, anywhere in the world." Tahiti had been her husband Tom's choice. She tossed the tickets off the desk.

She closed her eyes, imagining what the next three months held, and she saw nothing. No white sand, no walking hand-in-hand, nothing. Everyone knew the partners had a couple of new projects lined up when she got back; all she had to do was choose one. She pushed the first button on the phone and said, "Karen, is everything set for tomorrow?"

"Yes, ma'am, everything. You need to go home, get some sleep, and look fabulous tomorrow. "

"Karen, as always, you are right."

Heather tossed her jacket over her shoulder, picked up her pumps in one hand, draped her purse over the other shoulder and headed out the door, turning the lights off as she exited.

Karen was holding a suit in a new bag as she walked out her office door, and said, "A new suit. I had the tailor start with a size smaller and then do all your regular adjustments. It's for tomorrow's ribbon cutting."

Heather took the suit and said, "If anyone ever offers you another job, consider your salary doubled." Karen always tried to please, and her smile expressed her pleasure.

Heather walked down the hall, looking over the cubicles of the young architects and engineers. She turned the corner and saw a poster of a twelfth-century castle, with a tall distinguished looking man standing on the drawbridge staring straight at her with piercing deep blue eyes. He had something in his hand. She had a hard time figuring out what it was. She stopped and stared at the poster.

"Mrs. Wilson, may I help you?" A young voice asked.

Heather looked down at the young man, but didn't reply.

He repeated himself and said, "Mrs. Wilson, is there something wrong?"

She said, "Jordon, Jordon Phillips, right?"

"Yes, ma'am, I… I… I am impressed you remembered me from the interview. Today is my first day."

"I'm a Berkeley graduate myself. We Bears tend to stick together around here. We have to keep those Cardinals on their toes." She paused and then said, "Where did you get that poster?"

"It's a photo I took while visiting my uncle in Germany. I had it blown up to poster size."

"Is the castle from the Twelfth Century?"

"Yes, how did you…? Of course you would know that, yes, it is the *Landeck* Castle. Actually, my uncle tells me it is called

Burg Landeck – *burg* meaning 'castle'. The man in the picture is my uncle. He has lived over there for 20 years."

"Where did you fly into when you visited him?"

"Frankfurt."

She stared at the poster and said, "Frankfurt. Are you going to the ribbon cutting ceremony, tomorrow?"

"I didn't know I could."

She smiled and said, "Yeah, everyone in the firm will be there."

"Then I'll be there, too."

She looked at the poster again. There was something about that castle, about those eyes. Still in her stocking feet, she decided to take the stairs down to the parking garage rather than the elevator. She had spent too much time at her desk of late. She slipped on her shoes as she entered the parking garage and walked over to her BMW M3. Tom had wanted the M3 in the divorce. She wouldn't budge, so instead he got the house and alimony payments.

She got into the M3 and closed her eyes. Suddenly she saw the castle from the poster. She opened her eyes again, started the M3, and drove to her new home. Once inside she stood and looked at her barren apartment. She simply did not have time to make it feel like a home. There was just the most basic of furniture, no paintings or art. She warmed up a frozen dinner and poured herself a glass of wine. Taking both to the coffee table by the couch, she put on some music, started to eat her meal, drifted off to sleep, and the dream began. She was in a horse drawn carriage pulling up to the *Landeck* Castle. It was dark and the moon gave the castle walls an eerie glow. She was pulled from the carriage and hurried through the castle gate. The urgency with which she was rushed inside the castle walls under the cover of darkness made her feel like a thief in the night, like someone who didn't belong. With the same sense of urgency, she was pushed up the stairs to a spacious and well-appointed room. Her things were placed neatly by a chest, and then the door shut and locked.

She felt alone and afraid. She gathered her belongings around her for comfort and curled up in the bed, fighting sleep, then waking, startled by those eyes staring at her…

Heather Wilson woke from her sleep with a start. Her heart was pumping and her breath was short. She quickly realized where she was: in her apartment, a bottle of wine on the coffee table. She stood and walked to the kitchen, placed the bottle of wine in the cellar unit, and said, "Enough of this."

She dressed for bed in a loose fitting nightshirt and then drifted off to sleep. She had vivid dreams that made little sense: the castle, the eyes, and then a soft touch … and those eyes! The feel of the touch woke her with a sensation of loving, care, and warmth.

Heather woke early. She had a big day ahead of her, but she couldn't get the strange dreams out of her head. She showered and dressed, choosing to pull her wild hair back in a tight bun for the presentation.

The ribbon-cutting ceremony went extremely well, just as she had planned. While the guests were enjoying the catered food, she saw the new architect, Jordon, and made her way though the crowd to him.

"So, Jordon, what did you think of the ceremony?"

Jordon was taking a sip of his drink and gulped hard. "It was good, Mrs. Wilson."

"Jordon, would you mind if I spoke to you in private?"

"Not at all, Mrs. Wilson."

"Exactly where is that castle in your picture?"

"It is in southern Germany near the border of France – about a two hour drive from the Frankfurt airport." He gave her further details of the roads and towns it was near.

After the ceremony, Heather called Karen and said, "You know my tickets to Tahiti?"

Karen said half kidding, "Please, oh, please, tell me you have decided to go and are taking me."

"No, not quite, but I was wondering if you could turn them in for vouchers and book me on a plane to Frankfurt next week. I have decided to take that three months leave after all."

CHAPTER TWO
GETTING AWAY

Heather normally spent months planning trips; she would craft detailed itineraries, deciding where she was going to go, what she was going to do, plan activities for Tom, and make sure her parents were okay. But this time she was going alone. It was the first vacation she had ever taken by herself. She almost talked herself out of the trip, but then she would have those dreams of castles, knights, and those deep blue eyes.

She plotted a course from Frankfurt International Airport to the *Landeck* Castle. From there, who knew where she was going to go. She realized she would need to rent a car. She quickly looked up what it would take to rent a car in Germany, and found out that as a US citizen, an international driver's license would be helpful. She could get one from her local auto club.

Feeling more rushed and unprepared than she had ever felt on a trip, she arrived at the international terminal at San Francisco International Airport. Before getting out of the taxi, she checked her purse for her passport and ticket. The taxi driver pulled out her two backpack bags. She paid him and checked her bags at the American Airlines desk. She would fly to Chicago, and then from Chicago to Frankfurt.

With two long flights ahead of her, Heather was glad she had a break in Chicago to stretch her legs. Once airborne leaving Chicago she had her dinner, and before long, it was dark heading east. She tried to sleep, but sleep did not come easily. She was awakened when it was announced that they would be landing shortly in Frankfurt and to make sure the seatbacks were in an upright position and seatbelts fastened

Upon arrival in Frankfurt, Heather was suddenly confronted with a foreign language – German. In her haste to make this trip, it didn't even occur to her that she might be faced with a problem in communication. Although most of the airport personnel spoke English, as well as the arriving passengers, the language by everyone else was definitely not English. She doubted her decision, but she was here and would make the best of it.

Once through customs and baggage claim, she proceeded to the car rental area. They were most helpful and also provided her with a detailed map to her destination. She noted at once that even directional signs were not in English, and she became a bit apprehensive as she made her way out of the parking lot. No, she would not endanger herself or others on the highway because of ignorance. She must at least review road signs and their meaning.

She pulled off the highway into a parking area and reviewed the packet of material she had been given by the rental agency. She was pleased to see that driving rules and regulations were there, and she began a ten-minute crash course in driver sign recognition. She learned that 'exit' was *Ausfahrt* and 'entrance' was *Einfahrt*, plus a few other important things she needed to know, and she was again on her way.

Germany's high-speed roadway, the Autobahn, required her complete driving concentration. Once she had navigated onto the right road, she settled back and realized how far from home she was. She was amazed at the beauty of the green fields separating villages. The quaint looking houses with their tiled roofs looked solidly built and reminded her of pictures she had seen and books she had read. She kept focused on the road signs, which were clearly marked, and was pleased that she had not made any wrong turns. At first she was startled when cars in the left hand lane passed her as though she were standing still. Then she remembered that there were no speed limits except where posted. As she made her way further south, she noticed the many vineyards typical of the Palatine wine region as she approached the town of Neustadt *an der Weinstrasse*. Off to her right in the distance was a forested mountain range; she knew it was there that she would find her castle.

Once she passed through Landau she saw the sign to Klingenmünster. The two-hour drive had passed quickly, and her heart raced a bit with anticipation. Each village was surrounded by vineyards, which also made her curious about the wine in this region. As she approached the village of Klingenmünster, she saw the castle sitting majestically above the town. It had a strategic location that commanded a wide view of the surrounding area.

She drove through the village and followed the directional signs to the castle. It was a narrow road leading upward, and the closer she got to the castle, she felt some magnetism: as though something was drawing her to it. The parking lot was completely deserted; in fact, she didn't see anyone with the exception of a lone figure standing on the bridge leading into the castle. She parked and stood briefly by her car taking in the view of the castle and the surrounding area. She watched the solitary figure standing on the bridge as she began making her way. She stopped. She felt him staring at her.

***

He stood on the wooden bridge overlooking the moat. It was not the first time that he had come here. He was drawn to *Burg Landeck* seemingly by some unknown force, and it had become a place for him to escape the humdrum of daily life. It also provided time to sort out problems and reflect on his often adventurous past. His mother was a native German from the Palatine (Pfalz) region who had met his father when he was stationed at Ramstein Air Force Base. Their courtship was brief and they were married just before his father was scheduled to return to America for discharge from military service. Hans had visited Germany often over the years to visit his grandparents. It was during that time that he became fascinated with the castles in the Pfalz region. After his studies were completed, he spent his summer vacation in Germany and met his future wife while hiking in the *Pfälzerwald*. When they married, they agreed that upon retirement they would settle in Germany. He had been self-employed for the latter part of his career as an international business consultant and that allowed him to retire at an early age.

The perpetual struggle to achieve had been the driving force that took him from North America, to Europe, and then to the Middle East. Now all he had were memories. His retirement to Germany had fulfilled his promise and a lifelong dream, until it was shattered.

As he stood there gazing at his surroundings, he noticed the arrival of a small car in the parking area. That was rather unusual at this time of day. He always came here when he could be alone, and the parking lot usually remained empty. The driver exited the car and began walking toward the castle. As the figure drew closer, he noticed that it was a woman. She picked her way steadily along the beaten path, and from time to time would stop and take in the surroundings. She had a full head of hair and the breeze caused her to brush it back from her eyes as she continued her approach. The sun reflected a reddish sheen on her head that changed from darker to lighter colors with the intensity of the light. His attention was now fixed on this woman whose stature was remarkably tall. She walked with athletic prowess – almost cat-like.

As she neared the castle, he turned his head away, but kept her in view from the corner of his eye. His fascination made him wonder why she would be coming to the castle alone at this time of day. She walked as with a purpose, and as she came into view, she stopped abruptly and looked up at him. Their eyes met. It was still some distance away, but there was no mistake about it. Their eyes locked on each other. After a few moments, she continued her advance toward the castle. Where he stood, she would pass right by him. He thought briefly of moving away, but then he couldn't resist having a closer look.

She stepped onto the bridge, and although she walked on its wooden planks, the normal sound of footsteps echoing on the castle walls was not heard. She wore soft-soled athletic-type shoes that enabled her to move without making a sound. As she came within three steps from where he stood, he bowed his head slightly and said, "*Guten Morgen.*"

She looked puzzled, and then he said, "*Bonjour*" Looking at the perplexed smile on her face and seeing her shaking her head, he finally said, "Good Morning?" She continued smiling and extended her hand saying, "Good morning."

As they shook hands she stared into his eyes, and then whispered, "You are he."

He was surprised by her comment, searching his memory, trying to remember if they had ever met. The blue eyes seemed so familiar…but no, he would have remembered those wild curls of red and her height. No, he was sure. He would have remembered her. He responded, "I believe you've mistaken me for someone else."

"No, I am certain. You are the man in the picture. I don't mean to seem forward, but is Jordon Phillips your nephew?"

Surprised by her question he said, "Yes, yes, he's my sister's son." As a youth, Jordon had spent numerous summers with him in Europe; he was almost like a son, and as adults they exchanged emails on a regular basis. Suddenly he was worried; he immediately recognized her accent. Why had this American woman driven straight to the castle as if on a mission? Was there something wrong with Jordon?

"How do you know him? Is he all right?"

"Yes, he is fine, and a very bright and talented young man, if I might add. He was my top pick of our graduate hires this year."

Beaming with pride, the man said, "Jordon has always been interested in architecture. You must be with Kranshaw, Martin, and Wilson. Jordon told me that he secured a position with one of the top firms in San Francisco."

She smiled with a twinkle in her eyes as she said, "I like to think we are the best firm." She paused and then said, "How rude of me. I'm Heather Wilson."

He replied, "I'm Johann Hess."

There was an awkward moment of silence while his eyes remained fixed on hers, and then he said, "So what brings you to the village of Klingenmünster, Mrs. Wilson?"

She replied, "It's Ms. Wilson, and I came to see this castle. I saw it on a poster in Jordon's office and I just had to come and see it, in person." She turned and looked down at the bridge, and whispered in a low moan, "Oh, yes." Catching her breath, she whispered, "Look at those arches, classic 12th century. To see them in person."

The tone of her voice, the passion of her whisper, took him by surprise, finally he said, "I take it you are familiar with architecture of this period?"

She replied, "Yes. Yes, I am, but only through my studies. I have always loved the architecture of this period. I drew pictures of castles when I was a child, studied them in school, but there was never time to see them in person." She touched the drawbridge rail and said, "This is not original. The edges are too sharp, too finely cut, modern; within the last twenty years."

"Much of the castle has been renovated. It is considered a *Ruine*. It is one of the many ruins in the *Pfälzerwald*, the forest of the German Palatinate. Most every castle in this region was destroyed in past wars over the centuries. This and others in this region were destroyed by the French in the 17th century."

She slowly walked along the bridge to the arches. He didn't know if he should follow, but he couldn't help himself. She seemed mesmerized by the arches leading into the castle. Then she touched the stone, and said, "Oh, now this is original. I can tell by the texture of the grout."

She turned around and said, "Come, come feel this stone."

He stepped next to her. She took his hand, placing it firmly on the stone, and while holding it there said, "Feel the texture."

Their eyes made contact. Suddenly he felt catapulted to another time. He felt his hand holding her hand forcefully against the castle wall and looked at her longingly. She was wearing 12th century clothing, a long white gown with royal blue ribbons, tight bodice forcing her amble breasts upward, and a head covering that framed her wild red curls. In the vision, he could smell her fragrance enticing him as he forcefully kissed her. He felt the softness of her lips, the trembling of her body, as she slowly yielded to his kiss. He released her hand from the wall. She jumped back and away from him at the same moment and the vision was gone. They turned, eyes diverted from one another.

After an awkward moment of silence she said, "I am sorry I have taken so much of your time, Mr. Hess." She turned and quickly walked inside the castle away from him.

He stood for a moment, somewhat bewildered. This castle had always drawn him in, but that vision felt real, as real as her hand on the wall.

He turned, crossed over the bridge and took the long way home, walking along familiar trails through the forest. His walks were his time for reflection, peace, and appreciating nature. The spring colors with the bright leaves were almost gone. Normally he enjoyed nature, but today he was distracted by the strange encounter with the American woman. He walked directly to the *Pfalzklinik* health care facility located just below the castle. The nurse Gretchen was as always at the front window. He asked, *"Ist sie schon wach?"* (Is she awake yet?)

Gretchen replied, "*Noch nicht, Herr Hess.*" (Not yet, Mr. Hess.) She buzzed the door.

"*Danke,*Gretchen." (*Thanks.)*

He walked through the facility to his wife's room. It was already five years since she had gone into a coma. At first she appeared to be suffering from neurological problems and had been sent to this facility. Then she had lapsed into the coma. She was no longer a young woman and her chances of waking from the coma diminished with each year.

CHAPTER THREE
THE NOTE

Heather Wilson could not get the feeling out of her mind, the feeling of his hand over hers, their eyes locked. She especially couldn't get that vision out of her mind, the forcefulness of his hand locked on hers, holding her against the wall, his strong body pressing against hers and the moisture of his lips kissing hers. At first she fought it, but his kiss persuaded her, his fragrance embraced her, and she trembled with apprehension and anticipation, and then yielded as he released his hold. She felt the soft velvet of the royal blue tunic as she wrapped her hand around his waist. Their hands broke away, and then the vision was gone.

She wondered, had he felt it, too? Was that why he broke away so suddenly? She thought about him, his eyes deep blue, his face wise yet sad, his hands strong, his stature tall and his body solid. She knew he was older than her, but how much was hard to tell. Besides, she preferred older men. Heather was surprised by her thoughts, she hadn't though of any man in a romantic way since she walked in on her husband, until today.

What was she thinking, asking a complete stranger to feel the stone on the castle? With the deliberate speed at which he walked away, she was sure he may contemplate going somewhere and talk about this crazy American who grabs complete strangers hands and tells them to feel castle mortar.

She tried to push the thoughts from her mind as she explored the castle. The fortress was an irregular oval shape that conformed to the hilltop. A tall square tower stood just to the right of the archways and bridge that spanned a moat.

There were various signs that described the purpose and function of the rooms and areas, but they were all in German, and using her German-English dictionary was painful and arduous. Foreign language had never been one of her strong suits.

Despite her frustration, she loved the feel, the look and everything about the castle. She had lunch by the fireplace at the small café within the castle walls, and then continued to explore the castle. She had focused on the ground level rooms and chambers at first, saving the tower for the late afternoon.

As she was exploring the tower, she sat on a stone bench next to a window with a view of the valley. She was taking in the feel and function of this unique space. She placed her hand over the edge of the bench, and she felt something strange. It wasn't stone, as she expected, or even the unique feel of mortar, but it felt crisp, like paper.

She allowed her fingers to explore this strange substance. She explored the end of the paper, and, while touching a piece of mortar next to it, the paper fell into her hands. Surprised, she pulled her hand out from under the bench where she sat, and saw the very carefully rolled up piece of paper. Good sense told her to try and put it back into its slot, but curiosity got the best of her and she slowly unrolled it, taking utmost care not to damage it in any way. Her eyes opened wide when she saw the ink still very much intact, but she couldn't read it. She noticed that the paper was actually a parchment or vellum that had been preserved in the clay-like mortar. It was written in some language that she did not know. She knew she should put it back, but resisted the urge and just held onto it.

She took the stairs down the tower, and then walked out of the castle and to her car. She had made reservations at a quaint bed and breakfast called La Cava, located in Göcklingen, a neighboring town.

That night Heather dreamed of the castle, of the note, and of the man with the deep blue eyes. She woke the next morning somewhat tired. The jet lag, with nine hours time difference to California, was having its affect. She showered and went down to breakfast. It really was rather quaint seeing that breakfast was served just for guests. The small Bed and Breakfast, called a *pension* did not have a full time restaurant, but was open to the public for dinner on specified days. Food was provided to guests for all desired meals. Having breakfast on the outside patio was very pleasant.

She listened to conversations in German, wishing she had spent more time learning the language before she made her trip. Then she saw Mr. Hess walking past the pension with a newspaper under his arm. Without any thought, she waved to get his attention. He noticed the wave, hesitated, and then stopped. As though considering what to do next, he came to her table.

"Good morning, Ms. Wilson. I trust you had a good rest?"

"Yes, I did, and thank you for asking. Will you join me for a cup of coffee?"

"I'd be pleased," he said and sat down. When the waitress came, he ordered in German. From hearing his German and their conversation of the previous day, she knew he was fluent in both German and English. She could spend days finding a guide that would take her around, or she could be bold once again and ask Mr. Hess to at least help her find a guide.

"Mr. Hess, could I ask you a very big favor?"

He looked over his glasses and said, "A favor?"

"A business proposition. I need a guide. Could you help me find one, someone who speaks German and English?"

"What type of guide are you looking for?"

Somewhat relieved that he hadn't told her to leave him alone, she said, "Someone to go up to the castle with me to read the signs and help me order off menus."

He looked at her rather puzzled and said, "You came to Germany and you don't know any German?"

"None," she confessed.

He shook his head while smiling, and said, "That is a common thing, especially for Americans who expect everyone to speak English." He folded his paper. "If you remain here until 10:30 a.m., your guide will be waiting."

Heather was excited that she would finally be able to learn more about the castle. She felt she had only scratched the surface. She paced her room in anticipation. She pulled out the note she had slipped into her purse and felt the parchment; she looked at the words and wondered what secret mystery they held. Finally at 10:15 she went downstairs, and waited. At exactly 10:30 Mr. Hess walked up.

She said, "Have you found a guide for me?"

He smiled. It was perhaps the first time she had seen him smile, and he said, "You are looking at him."

"I can't impose on you. I'm sure you have other things to do, a job."

"I am a retired businessman. Are you ready?" He looked down at her feet and said, "Good, you'll need good walking shoes."

"Walking shoes?" she asked, as he turned and started walking to the street. She caught up with him and said, "I thought we were going to the castle."

"We are. We're walking."

She fell in stride with him as they walked through town and then onto a path through the vineyards. He explained that all the villages in this area were wine villages, referred to as

Weinorte, and that it was a famous wine region called the *Südliche Weinstrasse*.

The path they took led them to the foot of the mountain and the trail led into the forest. There was little conversation except for chatter about other points of interest. Then he said, "I emailed my nephew."

"You did? How is Jordon?"

"He is fine." And then he added, "I asked him why some woman would show up in Germany, not knowing the language, without a guide or being part of a tour."

She had to walk fast to keep up with him as he began the climb up the trail. "And what did he say?" She asked.

"He told me that you are a senior member of the firm on a three month leave, after completing the most important project in the firm's history. He mentioned that there was rumor that the project cost you your marriage. Jordon was concerned that his poster may have been the catalyst for your sudden departure to Germany. As such, he feels somewhat responsible that you came to Germany unprepared, and, at his request, I agreed to be your guide."

She stopped in her tracks and said, "Excuse me, I'll have you know I am quite capable of taking care of myself. I offered to pay someone to be my guide!"

"My services as your guide are not for free, I will expect something from you in return."

Expect something, she thought. Suddenly she realized how vulnerable she was, a woman, walking on a secluded trail with a man she had just met the day before, in a foreign country where she didn't know the language. She had been forward in their meetings, in a way that could have easily been misinterpreted. She stopped walking, inspecting her surroundings, the terrain, paths for escape. She needed to set the record straight and she said, "Mr. Hess, I will gladly pay you handsomely for your services, but if you think I. . . "

He interrupted her and said, "If I think you don't know the language and plan to spend the next three months here, I would be right. What I expect from you, Ms. Wilson, is to learn the language as we go, so that you can travel and get along in this country."

She felt such the fool for misinterpreting Mr. Hess' words. Perhaps it was the vision that she saw the previous day that made her think he was interested in her in some other way. No, he was an American who had lived in Germany for the last twenty years and probably felt just a little embarrassed by Americans who arrogantly went to another country assuming that everyone spoke English. She watched as he continued up the hill. No, she had something to prove to this man. She wasn't going to be the typical ugly American. She was going to learn the language, appreciate the culture, and get to know the people, starting with Johann Hess.

CHAPTER FOUR
THE GUIDE

Johann hiked to the top of the hill. He had walked this hill many times and knew the path well. He knew where the path was uneven, where tree roots stuck out. He set a quick pace. He didn't know why, but he wanted to test the American woman architect. He remembered how she walked up the hill the first time he saw her, with an athletic gait, yet quiet, cat-like. He wondered if she could keep these traits if he pushed the pace. He was impressed when he saw her right behind him the entire way up the hill.

As they came to the stone entrance, he produced a printout from a website that described the castle, which he had printed after deciding to be her guide. He opened the sheet, holding it out. She stood near him, able to read off the sheet. He could smell the freshness of shampoo. He liked having her standing close.

He followed the words on the paper with his finger, and said, "This first sentence says, *'Die Burg Landeck gilt als eine der schönsten Stauferburgen der Pfalz'*, which means, 'the castle *Landeck* is considered as one of the most beautiful Staufen era castle-forts of the Palatine'."

She attempted to repeat Mr. Hess' words as she read along, and said, *"Die Burg Landeck gilt als eine der schönsten Stauferburgen der Pfalz."*

He smiled and said, "We will need to work on your accent, but that was a good start."

Then she attempted to read it again, interpreting it in English as she went, "*Die Burg Landeck* - the castle *Landeck*. So *die* is 'the'." She smiled and said, "I think I can handle that."

He smiled. He liked her smile.

"So does that mean *Burg* is castle?"

"Yes, more accurately, a castle-fort. Don't confuse them with palatial castles like *Neuschwanstein* – or Walt Disney!" he grinned. "The word for those is *Schloss*."

Her face lit up and she said, "Wow, that makes so much sense. All these town names like Hamburg are towns with castles."

He nodded and said, "Continue."

Then she said, "*Gilt als*, 'considered as'." She looked up with her blue eyes and he nodded, knowing the *gilt als* could also mean 'applies as', but not in the context of this sentence. They were details that would only confuse her at this point, so he nodded, allowing her to continue. The she said, "*Eine* – 'one'. I actually remember that from grammar school! *Die* – 'the', *schönsten* – does it mean 'beautiful'?"

He replied looking into her eyes, "Actually, *schönsten* means 'most beautiful'." And as he said the words, the sun glistened off her red hair, her deep blue eyes, and he wasn't sure if he was speaking of the castle or her - or both.

"What an interesting people and a wonderful language to have a single word for 'most beautiful': *schönsten*. In a place so beautiful, how can one be sure that something is the most beautiful?"

He stared at her, realizing he liked her insight. They walked through the arches and then into the main courtyard, both of them avoiding contact with the wall they had felt the day before. Once inside the courtyard he said, "Let's go to the chambers first."

He led her down to the lower chambers reading from signs and then translating and then having her repeat his translation. She seemed eager to learn, which pleased him. As they moved from area to area, she would describe or explain unique architectural features. Although he was the guide, he felt he was also learning from her. They had lunch at the restaurant within the castle, in the open air.

After finishing lunch, they walked across the courtyard and he said, "This is where they hosted festivals, here in the courtyard." Their shoulders touched as they walked past a group of people, and just as the previous day, he felt thrown, for just a brief moment, to another time, dancing in a group in the courtyard, his shoulder touching hers. She was wearing the same white dress with blue ribbons, and he was in his royal blue tunic. Yet unlike the day before, the moment was brief, only a second. The two quickly moved away from one another as they continued their tour of the castle.

As the sun sank in the afternoon, Johann didn't want the day to end, but he had other responsibilities. He finally said, "Ms. Wilson, I must take my leave. I hope you have found my guidance helpful. I would suggest that you pick up some tapes to help with the tone and dialect, but I am pleased with the way you are translating words."

She smiled and said, "I have a very good teacher. I truly appreciate the time you have given to me."

They left the castle in the late afternoon and walked down though the forest, along the paths through the vineyards, into the village and to her pension.

She hesitated and then said, "Mr. Hess, how are you with some of the older languages?"

"I have spent some time learning some root languages that helped me speak some other modern languages in the business world," he replied.

She looked at him, hesitated briefly, and then said, "I have a bit of a mystery, actually, a note that I found. I don't recognize the language. I was wondering if you might join me for dinner and I could show you the note."

Johann was surprised by the invitation. He had truly enjoyed spending the day with Ms. Wilson. He wondered if she had read something more into their arrangement, or was he feeling something more and reading that into her invitation.

She said, "I'm so sorry, Mr. Hess. I didn't mean to be so forward. I was just hoping that you could help me solve a bit of a mystery while at the same time continuing my lessons on ordering meals. It will be my treat."

"I would be happy to continue your lessons and you need not treat. I'll see you at seven p.m."

Heather quickly showered. She went through her clothes several times wondering where they would go for dinner, and what she should wear. She finally decided on a simple sweater set and a pair of slacks. For all she knew, Mr. Hess might choose a restaurant where they would have to walk a couple of miles. She switched from her more dressy slip-on shoes to a more practical loafer.

She pulled the note out and slipped it into her purse. Perhaps he might be able to decipher it.

At 6:45 p.m. she headed down to the lobby and paced the floor. She was actually excited and apprehensive about the dinner. Mr. Hess had been a wonderful instructor, pleasant, mannerly, and at the same time distant. There were times when he let his shield down and smiled, a smile that made her feel so good. But then he would slip back into his shell, remaining distant. In fact, he had grown more aloof after they touched in the courtyard and she had yet another brief vision, this time of them dancing in an old group dance. Perhaps it was a just a daydream. Perhaps it was more, but there were times when she felt a closeness to him that she hadn't felt in a long, long time.

Suddenly she started to wonder why he seemed so distant at times. Is it just his nature or was there another reason? Suddenly she thought to herself, "What if he is married?" The thought had never crossed her mind. She always saw him alone, alone in the photo in Jordon's office, alone on the day that she arrived and alone today.

Heather paced more intensely as she waited. She wondered, should she just ask him if he was married. But that would seem very forward. It wasn't as if he had made any romantic advances toward her. By asking if he were married, she would suddenly put herself in a position of suggesting that she had a romantic interest in him. And what if he was married? He had agreed to go to dinner with her; what then? Would that make her the other woman? No, even if he was married, he had been very professional. Heather decided that she would ask such a forward question if and only if he made a romantic play for her.

Heather was waiting when she saw a Mercedes pull up. She watched Mr. Hess get out of the car and walk up to the entrance. She noticed how handsome he looked in dress slacks and a blazer. She wondered if she was under-dressed. Mr. Hess said, "Evening, Ms. Wilson."

She replied, "*Abend* Mr. Hess."

He smiled, "You have been working on your German; I am impressed! Shall we go?"

They went to the car and he held the passenger door open for her. She got in and then he went around to the driver's side and got in. He said, "I thought we should go to the Poseidon in Landau. It's a Greek restaurant with an outstanding wine cellar. You do like wine, don't you, Ms. Wilson?"

She smiled and said, "Yes, I do. I used to go the vineyards in Napa Valley all the time."

"I have heard of their wine," he said.

Landau was just eight kilometers away; the time passed quickly. Mr. Hess said, "This is the main shopping area of the region. There are all types of shops just up the road from here. You may be able to find a couple of book stores with some English to German tapes." They pulled into the restaurant's private park area, and, as he had done at the pension, he opened her door and extended his hand to assist her out of the car. Then he took her arm and they walked into the restaurant.

There were two eating areas. One was on the main floor, but the larger dinning area was in the basement. As he led her down the stairway, the smell of food made her mouth water. She couldn't wait to see the menu. As they entered the room, the massive stone arches drew her immediate attention. She hesitated a moment to observe the architecture with its stone walls and stone floor; even the ceiling was constructed of stone. The place was wonderful.

Mr. Hess spoke to the headwaiter, exchanging some pleasantries in German, and then they were ushered to a quiet corner alcove. Heather found the place absolutely charming. Once seated, she felt like they were in their own private world.

The waiter came, and Mr. Hess ordered wine. After the waiter left he asked, "So what do you think of the Poseidon?"

"The food smells fabulous; the architecture of this place is wonderful."

"I thought you might like the architecture," he said smiling pleasantly.

The waiter came and poured wine into Mr. Hess' glass. Heather watched as Mr. Hess lifted the glass, looked at the color, and then swirled it in the glass, taking in the aroma before taking a sip. He let it sit in his mouth for a moment, swallowed and then nodded. As he took a sip, she noticed the simple wedding band on his left ring finger. He was married.

The waiter poured the wine into two glasses, and her dinner companion offered up a toast, "To you, Ms. Wilson, may you continue to be as good a student as you have been today." She marveled at the way he carried himself; he did everything with style and class. It was too bad he was married.

She said, "To you, Mr. Hess. I have a good instructor," They took another sip of wine and then she said, "You know, most people call me Heather."

Then Mr. Hess said, "We shall make it formal. In Germany one refers to another person in a formal manner until it is agreed to become informal. The term *Sie* is used instead of the more familiar term *Du* when addressing other person. And *Herr* for 'Mr.' is used instead of the familiarity of a person's first name. In the case of a woman, we say *Frau*, or *Fraülein* if the female is unmarried, although that term is vanishing from the vocabulary. It is customary for young people to share a drink together when they advance from *Sie* to *Du*, and since, as an American, you are accustomed to using first names, perhaps we can use this nice ritual to formally make the switch."

He raised his glass and said, "To you, Heather,"

She replied, "To you, Johann."

He smiled and said, "Johann is a formal version of Hans. All my friends call me Hans."

Heather said, "To you, Hans." She liked the full flavor and richness of the wine. "This wine, is it from a local vineyard?"

"No, I thought since we would be eating Greek cuisine we would enjoy a Greek wine. They also have good wines in Greece. This is a "Makedonikos Landwein". You will have ample opportunity to enjoy our local wines, and I will make sure you become familiar with them," he said smiling.

They chatted briefly about the castle, and then a few minutes later the waiter came to take their order.

"Would you care to order yourself or would you mind if I order for you?"

"Oh, please do. I wouldn't know what I'd be ordering and you'd have to translate each item on the menu. But I would like you to teach me how to order."

"Always the willing student. In due time, in due time. For the moment, I'll order the following:

Gemischte Platten (Mixed Platter),

Mykonos-Teller (Myconos Plate),

1 Suflaki, 1 Suzuki mit Käse überbacken (cheese baked on top),

1 Steak mit Käsesauce und Pommes (with cheese sauce and fries),

Makedonikos Rotwein halbtrockener Landwein (Macedonian semi-dry red table wine)"

Heather listened to what he ordered and then they continued their discussions of the castle and of the restaurant. It seemed as if they had so much to share, and all along he would repeat words in German and she would do her best to duplicate his words.

He smiled quite a bit during the evening, and each time he did she felt herself drawing closer to him. She wondered if it was his wonderful smile or the wine or both. The dinner was served, and while they ate, they talked. After he ordered desert, she said, "Mr. Hess, I mean Hans, I had asked if you would look at this note I found."

"Yes, yes, you did. May I see it?"

She pulled the rolled up note from her purse and handed it to him. He placed on his reading glasses and looked at the note in the faint light. He seemed surprised as he unrolled it. He looked at her and said, "Yes, I recognize the language, it is written in an old German dialect commonly used among literate aristocrats up until the 1200s. Let me see if I can decipher it."

He looked at the writing and translated as he read, *"Tonight was a night of many surprises. The games were eventful as always and my favorite champion was wearing his colors of royal blue and gold. I watched his bravery in the games, his skill with the sword, the foil, and the lance. I wore my white dress with blue ribbons to show support for my favorite champion. He arrived wearing a dashing blue tunic."* He stopped.

Heather looked at him, dumbfounded, and said, "Is that all?"

With his eyes diverted, he said, "No, there is more."

She asked, "Could you read it, please?"

He continued, *"There was the dance. We actually met in a Quadrille, where our hands touched as we danced with other dancers. After the dance, feeling faint I walked out to the drawbridge for some fresh air. He walked me to the gate. As we stood in the arches, he grabbed my hand, and then kissed me."*

"What type of joke is this you are playing on me, Ms. Wilson?"

She looked at him somewhat perplexed and said, "Whatever do you mean, Hans?"

He stared at her, and then said, "The white dress with blue ribbons, the dance, the kiss. What kind of games are you playing?"

She stared at him, "You saw the vision too?"

He folded his napkin. "I have no idea what you are talking about!"

"Yes, you do. You saw those visions, of the couple dancing, of the kiss at the wall."

His eyes were piercing as he looked at her and said, "What kind of trickery is this?"

She said, "I could ask you the same question; you are reading the note. Do you think I could have written that, in that language? Speaking of which, does it say anything else?"

He looked at the note and read, *"Next month we travel to Madenburg for the games there. I hope I see my champion again."*

Heather stared at him and said, "Well, I guess that tells me where I am going next."

"What will you do, search for another note? And who will translate it for you?"

"I was hoping you would accompany me to *Madenburg*, unless, of course, you are too busy, or your wife is waiting for you at home."

He paused before replying, and then said, "No, my wife is not at home any longer; there is no one waiting for me at home."

By the sadness in his eyes, Heather could tell she had broached a difficult subject. Given his age and the sadness in his eyes, she suspected that his wife had passed.

Their dessert arrived, but neither ate much. Nothing much was said as they drove back to her pension. As he got out of the car and opened her door, he said, "I have something to do tomorrow, but the following day I will take you to the *Madenburg*." He walked her to her pension, opened the door for her, and then returned to his car.

Heather was surprised. She stood there for a moment, holding the note in her hand. There was no doubt about it: she had seen visions of this young couple, and Hans Hess was a big part of that vision. What's more, he had no one at home waiting for him. She smiled.

CHAPTER FIVE
THE ORIGINAL NOTE

Hans watched Heather walk up the stairs to her room. His feelings towards this woman were growing stronger by the hour. She was passionate about her architecture and he enjoyed listening to her point of view about all the castles in the region, but there was more. Her willingness to learn appealed to him in a way that was hard to explain. He knew what it was. The vision made him realize what he was missing in his life. He was not a young man any longer, and although the desire had still been there, it faded when his wife went into a coma. He had thought that was a closed chapter in his life.

Over the past two days with Heather, he felt more alive than he had felt in years. She had a way, a smile, a look, and a passion that revived senses that had been dormant for quite some time. But she was eighteen years younger. What would she see in him: a teacher, a guide, maybe? But there was something; perhaps he was reading too much into it. He had never lived life with a perhaps, or a what if. He had traveled the world in what some might call adventure while others called it risk taking. Yet he had made his fortune in business, and he had never looked back to the perhaps, the what-ifs, of the world.

He parked his car next to his house, a comfortable cottage with all the trappings of home. It had been his place to retire. It was a place where he and his wife would live out their golden years in peaceful bliss. That was before the problems started. Before her illness took effect. Then she had slipped into a coma. For the past few years he had been going through the motions.

He walked into his cottage and said, "Welcome home."

He practiced saying words in English when he was alone. He spoke so much German now that he felt the need to practice English just a little or he might forget it. He had been using his English more in the past two days than he had in months before. It was nice talking to Heather in English.

He thought about the end of their evening, the way she brought up his wife. Didn't she know his wife was in a clinic? Perhaps Jordon had not filled her in on the severity of his wife's condition.

He was surprised by her decision to go to *Madenburg*. She was on a quest that the note had started. The context of the note frightened him to the core. It was as if the note was reading his mind. The visions felt so real, as though he was reliving the experience himself. Could it be? Could he be feeling the visions recorded on the paper?

He hoped against hope that it was not the case. He opened the top drawer of his dresser. On the top was a napkin that he carefully unfolded. Inside the folded napkin was a parchment of paper, tightly rolled, just like the paper Heather had found. He unrolled the paper and read the passage, which he had transcribed to memory. It was the same style, the same handwriting. He was convinced now more than ever that Heather had found the clue he had been looking for all these years.

And if those visions felt as real as they did, the context of his note frightened him. He rolled up the note and folded it back in the napkin.

That night Hans dreamed of dancing with Heather in his arms as they glided across the floor. It was a happy dream full of promise and expectation.

He awoke the next morning full of life. He picked flowers on the way to the *Pfalzklinik*, creating a beautiful bouquet.

Nurse Gretchen was at the front window as usual. He asked, *"Ist sie schon wach?"*

"Noch nicht, Herr Hess."

"You know it is our anniversary today."

Gretchen smiled and said, "Herr Hess, you are the most romantic man I know," as she buzzed the door.

"Danke, Gretchen."

He walked through the facility to his wife's room. He retrieved the vase he had stored under the bathroom sink, placed the flowers in and added some water. He sat the flowers next to her bed and spoke as if she were conscious and awake, saying, "Happy Anniversary." He watched her briefly and then said, "I can't believe that it has been forty years, my dear. It seems like just yesterday that we were young." Finally, just before he left, he said, "I think I might have found a clue to the note. I may be gone for a little while as I track it down. I will inquire about you every day, my dear."

With that, he bent down, gave his wife a kiss on the cheek, and left.

***

Heather spent the day shopping. Most of her clothes were two sizes too big. Besides, she didn't want to look like a tourist. She looked at the style of clothing worn by the women in the village and decided to purchase several outfits that would help her to blend in. She traveled to Landau using the same roads Hans had used the night before and continued to the shopping district, following the directions that Hans had provided. She easily found the large *Messeplatz* a large open area used for festival events. Surrounding the open square were numerous shops. The surface of the *Messeplatz* was completely covered with cobblestones that had been placed, one stone at a time, many years earlier. It was exciting to drive on the old cobblestone streets and wonder what conditions were like in the early days.

As she made her way from store to store, she tried using the German greetings Hans had taught her, knowing they might sound a bit funny. She found that people were pleasant and gave her a big smile at her efforts with the language.

Her mind wandered to Hans often throughout the day. He had helped her a lot in just a couple of days. Her confidence grew as she made her way in and around the city. Her thoughts about Hans continued while having lunch at a small sidewalk Café. It was pleasant sitting in the open air watching the pedestrians.

She returned to her pension early in the evening. There was a message from Hans saying that he would take her to *Madenburg* tomorrow.

As she prepared for bed, she looked again at the note she found. The visions flashed through her head and she slept with them on her mind. She dreamed that she was in a carriage traveling from *Landeck* to *Madenburg*. The view of the countryside was enchanting, adding to her excitement.

CHAPTER SIX
MADENBURG

The next morning, Heather went downstairs to have breakfast. Shortly after she sat down, Hans walked in carrying a backpack, and said, *"Morgen,* Heather."

She smiled and said, "Morning. It is so nice to see you, Hans."

He bowed and said, "I was thinking we could ride a bicycle to the castle, if that would be okay with you?"

She hesitated, and then said, "It has been some time, but I think it would be fun."

"Before we go, you may wish to review what I jotted down about the castle."

He handed Heather a sheet of paper and she began to read:

Not far from the small town of Eschbach, Madenburg rises from the cliffs of the mountain Rothenberg in the Pfälzer Rheinebene. Madenburg is mentioned for the first time in 1076.

In 1317 Madenburg Castle became a property of the counts of Leiningen. From the late 14th century a Burggemeinschaft, *a castle community, inhabited Madenburg. In 1470 the troops of Count Palatine Friedrich I., the Victorious, besieged and conquered the castle.*

When Bishop Georg of Speyer bought Madenburg Castle in 1516, the entire property was held by a single owner. In 1525, during the Peasants' War the castle was destroyed. It was rebuilt and renovated several times at the end of the 16th century.

Since the 30 Years' War the castle has been besieged and attacked many times. At the end of the 17th century, during the

Reunion War (War of Palatine Succession), French troops completely destroyed the castle.

"It is so sad when war destroys such wonderful structures. To me these structures are like art, and when any beautiful work of art is destroyed, it saddens me." Then she said, "Yet it is so exciting. I can't believe I'm actually visiting places that have such a history. I can't wait to investigate *Madenburg*. I wonder what other mysteries it will reveal."

Hans smiled, extended his hand and led her to the stand where two bikes where parked. Without another word, they mounted the bikes and began to pedal. The balance and movement was soon natural to Heather and it felt good to be riding again. They left the village, making their way through the vineyards and rolling hills. He rode alongside and said, "I trust you had a nice day yesterday."

"I went shopping and enjoyed it very much; I was actually able to converse with several people, thanks to you."

The castle loomed larger as they continued toward it. The hill became steep in places, and they got off and pushed the bikes until the road leveled off again. There was a parking area just below the castle where they secured their bikes to a tree, and then hiked the rest of the way.

Heather was amazed at the expansive castle that was built in different time periods. One could tell that the center was very old, but there were sections that were from the twelfth and fifteenth centuries. They strolled through the various sections, stopping often to examine old engravings. When they entered the large chamber in the center of the castle complex that had once been used for entertainment, Heather smiled and said, "Can't you almost hear the music of a grand ball here?"

Hans nodded, but didn't say anything. There were large columns that supported the room. At one point Heather put her hand on the column about the same time as Hans, and the two of them were whisked away to another time, dancing across the ballroom as a couple. They looked into each other's eyes, and he pulled her tighter in the vision, as they glided across the dance floor. Suddenly Heather felt Hans' hand on her waist, in the same way, the same feel as the vision. She didn't want the dance to end, but eventually it did.

This time they did not break from the hold, but held on briefly looking into each other's eyes. She knew at once that they had both seen the vision together.

Finally she asked, "Please, please tell me you felt that."

He nodded, "Yes, I must admit I did." Hans then removed his hand from her waist.

They continued their tour. Much like *Burg Landeck*, this castle also had a restaurant where they enjoyed lunch.

In the afternoon, Heather was once again on a mission looking for a little scrap of paper. Much to her dismay, it grew late much too soon. They walked back to the bikes, and as they were about to leave, Hans placed his hand over hers that were gripping the handlebars and said, "We can look again for the note tomorrow."

The bike ride back was glorious with the sun shinning over the valley, and since it was mostly all downhill, it seemed rather effortless. As they entered the village of Eschbach, they stopped at the fountain in village center. Hans used this pause to mention the relationship of this town to *Madenburg*. It was this town of Eschbach that had collected the taxes for the castle. The fountain was a meeting place and had been a main source of water for the townspeople and for travelers who would stop to water their horses.

When they reached Heather's pension, Hans asked, "Would you care to have dinner with me tonight?"

Heather smiled and, touching his hand, said, "That would be nice."

***

Dining out this time was at a fun and jovial restaurant with music playing in the background. The owners of this restaurant had encouraged Hans to start dating again. After customary pleasantries, they were seated at a cozy table.

Hans ordered some wine and it was delivered with a small basket of fresh bread. After tasting the wine and giving his approval, he then ordered dinner with Heather's agreement. By continuing to teach her German, they were able to fill normally awkward moments with lessons. They conversed in a free and easy manner that blended with the fun nature of the restaurant.

After they finished desert, the owner approached Heather and said, "I bet you didn't know that our friend Hans Hess is quite the singer."

Hans shook his head.

The owner continued in broken English, "We like it when he does American songs by Elvis Presley and when he does 'Du-Du'."

Heather smiled and looking Hans said, "So you do Elvis and 'Du-Du'. What exactly is 'Du-Du'?"

Hans shook his head again. He knew what the owner was trying to do, and it wasn't going to work.

The owner said, "He has a wonderful voice; you must hear it."

He saw Heather look over at him and say, "Really?" He knew he was cornered.

Hans said, "I don't think Ms. Wilson would be interested in my singing."

"Of course I would. Please, Hans."

The owner immediately noted the familiarity and said, "Yes, please, Hans." Then he winked.

Hans knew there was no way out. He stood up and walked over to where the musicians were playing and said, *"Du-Du."* He watched the band shuffle through the sheet music. When they finished playing the opening chords, he began to sing:

"Du, du liegst mir im Herzen,
Du, du liegst mir im Sinn,
Du, du machst mir viel Schmerzen,
Weißt nicht wie gut ich dir bin.
Ja, ja, ja, ja,
Weißt nicht wie gut ich dir bin.

> You, you are in my heart,
> You, you, in my thoughts too,
> You, you cause me much pain,
> Don't know how good I'm for you.
> Yes, yes, yes, yes,
> Don't know how good I'm for you.

So, so wie ich dich liebe,
So, so liebe auch mich,
Die, die zärtlichsten Triebe,
Fühl ich allein nur für dich.
Ja, ja, ja, ja,
Fühl ich allein nur für dich.

> As, as, much as I love you,
> As, as much love me please,
> The, the most tender desires,
> I feel only for you,

Yes, yes, yes, yes,
I feel only for you.

Doch, doch darf ich dir trauen,
Dir, dir mit leichtem Sinn?
Du, du darfst auf mich bauen,
Weißt ja wie gut ich dir bin.
Ja, ja, ja, ja,
Weißt ja wie gut ich dir bin.

Yet, yet how can I trust you,
You, you of fickle mind?
You, you can count on me too.
You know to you I'd be kind.
Yes, yes, yes, yes,
You know to you I'd be kind.

Und, und wenn in der Ferne,
Mir, mir dein Bild erscheint,
Dann, dann wünscht ich so gerne,
Daß uns die Liebe vereint.
Ja, ja, ja, ja,
Daß uns die Liebe vereint."

And, and when I am far away,
To me, me your picture appears,
Then, then I wish so much that
Love will unite you with me.
Yes, yes, yes, yes,
Love will unite you with me.

He saw Heather watching him; initially it was a teasing
smile as he started to sing. Then her whole expression

changed, first to surprise as his soft baritone voice sang out the melody of the songs, then to curiosity, wondering what the words meant. It was then that he decided to translate the words into English between stanzas. They made eye contact as he said the words in English. She was transfixed by his voice and the words.

As he finished the song, a band member said, "Do Elvis."

"Another day," he said and went back to the table while watching Heather's beautiful blue eyes fixed on him. He finally broke the silence and said, "Well, was it that bad?"

"No. Oh, no, not at all. Oh, my goodness, that was such a beautiful song and you have such a beautiful voice. I am impressed. You amaze me every day Hans."

The owner came over and said, "See I told you he has a good voice, does he not?"

"He has a wonderful voice," she said while looking at Hans.

The owner smiled and repeated her words, "Wonderful voice."

"Thank you so much for translating it into English. The sound of it was so beautiful, but understanding the words made it that much more meaningful. It is a very romantic song."

Hans blushed. "Before long, you will know the words, so I won't have to translate it for you."

"I hope you are right."

They said their good-byes to the owner and walked to her pension. As they walked she said, "I never figured that you would have such a wonderful voice."

Somewhat embarrassed, he said, "Thank you."

"I would like to hear your Elvis."

"And what Elvis song do you know?"

"*Heartbreak Hotel*, of course."

He smiled. "Not a bad choice."

When they reached the pension door, he asked, "Do you want to bike again tomorrow?"

"Yes, I would. One can see so much of the country that way. There was a perfect spot along the way that looked like a good place for a picnic. It was on the hill right before the forest."

"Consider it done. I'll make a picnic basket."

"I meant to ask you about the bells. I keep hearing bells ringing. I assume they are church bells, but why do they ring so much?"

"They ring for various reasons, but primarily to signal the time of day. You will hear a single 'gong' on the quarter-hour, two 'gongs' on the half hour, three 'gongs' for the three-quarter hour, and then four 'gongs' for the full hour. There is a slight pause, and then, with a slightly different tone, the bell will signal what hour it is. If it is three o'clock, for example, it will ring three times, and so on. It works on a twelve-hour time system. But there is something else that I found interesting when I first got here that has mostly to do with tradition. Every day at 11:00 am., the bells will ring constantly for at least two or three minutes. That is to notify the women working in the fields that it is time for them to head home to start preparing lunch."

"Do they still do that? I mean work in the fields?"

"Some, yes. Although there are not that many working in the fields these days, the tradition still continues with the ringing of the bells."

"I would assume, then, that the women prepare a big meal for lunch."

"Yes, they do. Lunch is the big meal of the day and it is usually a hot meal. Afterward, many will take a short nap before they go back to work, and in this area, they usually go back into the vineyards to work."

"So if they have the big meal for lunch, what do they eat then for dinner?"

"For dinner they usually have what you would call 'cold cuts'. Bread, of course, with assorted sandwich-type sliced meats and assorted cheeses. It varies by area, but it is essentially that. Wine or beer is usually served with the meals. On Sundays the bells ring indicating it is time to go to church. There is a Catholic and a Protestant church in most every village. Their call to worship is separate and the bells from each church will ring about 15 minutes before the start of service. You will also hear bells ringing when someone dies. It does take some getting used to, but after a while you really don't notice the bells that much."

"Actually, it sounds very nice. Traditional. I can remember hearing church bells ring when I was a kid growing up in a small village in Arizona. I don't think they do that anymore. You know, Hans, I have really enjoyed my time here and I'm learning a lot, but I feel so bad taking so much of your time."

"As I have said, I am retired, I have no one at home, I have the time, and I enjoy teaching." He hesitated and then said, "Teaching you German, while learning from you about architecture. It gives an old man purpose."

She smiled and said with conviction, "Hans Hess, I don't consider you an old man. The way you bike, hike, and sing, you are far from old in my book. I am working hard to keep up with you." Then she put her hand on his shoulder in a very loving gesture.

Hans could still feel her hand on his shoulder as he walked to his cottage.

CHAPTER SEVEN
THE PICNIC

The next morning Hans met Heather outside the pension at 10:00 a.m. He said, "I have our picnic basket in my backpack. Shall we go?"

She wore a new sweater and a pair of slacks that fit her better than the previous ones. Hans couldn't help but notice her nice figure in the new pants and top.

As he watched her on the bike, he didn't need visions to conjure up feelings that had, prior to this week, been passive. He felt young when he was around her. They biked along the narrow road to the base of the *Madenburg*. They secured the bikes at the base of the hill and then hiked the rest of the way as before.

They slowly made their way through the various chambers and then up to what would have been the quarters, more specifically, the guest quarters. They found a room on one of the upper levels with windows looking out to the west.

Heather sat down on a stone bench and Hans sat next to her. From where they sat it gave them a clear view of the surrounding area. Heather said, "This is just like at *Landeck*. Just like the spot where I found the first note."

She felt under the bench, her fingers following the grout line, and sure enough, she found another note that had been rolled up and placed into the spot where the grout had once been. She carefully worked the parchment out of its hiding place, and exclaimed, "Another note."

He nodded and said, "You found your note."

"Our note," she replied. "This is our adventure."

She placed the note in her pocket without saying anything further. Hans didn't know how to take her comment. They walked around the castle for a while, admiring the different periods of architecture, but in the early afternoon, she said, "I am getting hungry. Shall we have our picnic?"

They hiked back down to the bikes and rode to the mound on the hill just before the forest. He grabbed his backpack and they hiked across the field to the knoll.

He spread a blanket. Heather rummaged through all the items in the basket: an assortment of hard cheeses, crackers, wine, and strawberries, and placed them on the blanket. As they ate, they talked about the castle. The warmth of the sun and the wine made them drowsy.

"Would you mind too much if this old man rests his weary bones?" He asked.

"Not at all. I was thinking the same thing"

He lay down, allowing the sun to soak in. It felt good. Before long he was fast asleep. He dreamed of hearing the giggling voice of a girl running through the field. It was Heather as a young woman running towards this spot. She had a basket under her arm, and behind her was a younger man chasing her She took a blanket from her basket and placed it on the soft warm grass and he immediately flopped on it. She smiled and said, "You've wrinkled my blanket."

"Do tell." He replied with a mischievous grin.

"Tisk, tisk," she said. "What is it about you always having such thoughts?"

"I am but a man, in the presence of the most beautiful woman in the world. How could one not have such thoughts?"

"Well, you can put those thoughts away. I am not the type of woman who can be so easily swayed by your charms."

"You are but a girl who doesn't even begin to understand or know my charms."

She took a strawberry from the basket and said, "So says you."

Then she took a bite of the strawberry and he quickly bit the other end, the strawberry exploding in their mouths, their mouths touching, he completed the kiss, and responded, "So say I."

"You are nothing but a cad," she replied,

"And you agreed to go on a picnic with said cad," he retorted.

"It was only at the urging of my cousin. She said we made such a great looking couple dancing, so then when I received your note, she urged me to accept."

"She urged you to accept, did she now?" He said with a grin, "Well, maybe I should ask your cousin to picnic instead."

She reached out to slap him and he caught her hand in mid air. He placed his other hand behind her head, and then kissed her. Then he guided her from a sitting position to a laying position as they kissed. "You do something to me," he said. "I can barely eat or drink around you. I sometimes find it hard to breath. I look for you in the crowd at the games and on the dance floor. What kind of spell do you have on me?"

She replied softly, "The spell that says no. You are used to having your way with women."

He kissed her again, and felt her resistance weaken. "I would give them all up to be with you."

"You say that now until you have taken my virtue." She pushed him up and away from her. Then she stood up and said, "I think I should go back to the castle."

"Please, please just sit with me, I will be good, I promise. I just want to bask in the sun and your radiance for a while."

"You'll be good?"

"Knight's honor, I'll be good." She sat down and then he laid his head in her lap, looking up at the skies, and said, "Do

49

you ever wonder how many lovers have sat on this very spot, and how many lovers will?"

"You never let it rest, do you?"

"I am not talking in the physical, but in the spiritual. Think of it, like two souls traveling through time meeting here as different lovers over and over again."

The comment woke Hans from a deep sleep. It was almost dark. He felt Heather's hand in his. She woke a moment later.

They didn't make eye contact for a second, and then she said, "Well, did you have another vision?"

"Did you?"

"Of having a picnic here?"

"Yes."

"We should get going."

He stood up and said, "Yes, I think we should, too."

They biked back to her pension as the sun set, neither knew exactly how long they had slept. They barely spoke a word as he held the door open for her. Hans thought about making a date for dinner, but then decided against it.

***

Heather thought it odd that Hans rushed off without allowing them to make plans for dinner or arranging to get together the next day. She decided against going out to dinner herself and retired early. She tossed and turned all night, thinking of the romantic rambling of the younger Hans in her vision: "I am not talking in the physical, but in the spiritual. Think of it: like two souls traveling through time meeting here as different lovers over and over again." It was a unique concept, to say the least. It gave a visual to the term soul mates.

She woke the next morning and went down for breakfast. The hostess at the front desk gave her a note. She opened it and it said, "Called away on business. Hans Hess."

Her mind wondered and speculated. She thought he was retired. How could he be called away on business? Maybe it was something else and he just claimed it was business. She wondered if he was all right. As the day progressed, she arrived at the only logical conclusion; it was a convenient excuse to avoid seeing her again, and she knew it.

Perhaps he grew tired of her ramblings about architecture. Her ex-husband Tom certainly would have. Perhaps he grew weary of her continual obsession about the note. The note, she realized she still had the note. Indeed she had the note, but she could not decipher it on her own. But more likely, she thought that he was probably just tired of having to explain and read German signs and posters.

Heather returned to Landau to the shopping district. She easily found the large *Messeplatz* and decided to make a day of shopping. First on her list was a good English to German tape and tape player. She searched from shop to shop and finally found a bookstore with a variety of books, some even in English. There she sat and looked through the books of castles and architecture, some in English and others in German. She loved looking at the books and the stories of the various castles. She spent much of the day just looking through the books. There was so much she wanted to see and do while she was here.

In the back of her mind, she kept wishing that Hans was here to answer a question, translate a sentence, give his advice, make recommendations, and share in all the wonderful regional books. She finally decided to buy a German language tape, a good English to German dictionary, a couple of books on the castles of the region, and one book about the German Wine Route.

She stopped in a couple more shops, bought things for Karen back home, and then entered a Café for a coffee. All in all it was an enjoyable day, except for the fact that she kept thinking of Hans. As the evening set in, she drove back to her pension.

Hans tried to stay away. That was why he wrote the note saying he would be away on business, but he couldn't. He had watched her drive away in the morning. She had not packed her luggage, and so she wasn't leaving entirely. He wondered if that would not have been better. All day long he wondered where she had gone, what she was doing, how she was getting along without him. Some time during the day, he realized that she meant more to him that he cared to admit. Maybe it was the notes, the visions, or her energetic personality that made him feel young again. Yet the note that he had in his possession spoke of great sorrow. But what had Shakespeare said? "It's better to have loved and lost than to have never loved at all." He wondered if that also applied to loving again. Was there a second chance, for him, or for these two soul mates?

As she consumed his thoughts, he knew he had no choice. Good or bad, joy or sorrow, this was his destiny, their destiny. Whatever the case, he wasn't going to risk it again. He waited in the park reading a newspaper, waiting for her return.

When her car pulled up he went to meet her. As she was getting her purchases out of the car, he said, "Good evening, Heather."

She smiled and then said, "*Guten Abend*, Hans. How was your business?"

"Fine, good. I see you have been shopping."

"Mostly books." She pulled them out. "Although I did buy a few things for my friends back in the States."

He saw the top book in her stack and said, "The German Wine Route. Is that something that interests you?"

"I like wine. I like biking. How could one not be interested?"

"No more castles?"

"From what I have read, there are castles along the wine route. Besides, I think it best to enjoy the country in its fullest and not focus on just one thing."

"That's a good idea," he said, then added, "So do you plan on
doing this route alone?"

With a shy smile she said, "Unless I can talk a guide into joining me."

His heart was melting, but he tried to remain cool as he said, "It has been a long time since I have taken that route."

"Well, perhaps you should see it again."

"That would be nice. Perhaps we could meet for coffee and discuss it."

"I would like that."

"Tomorrow in the morning, then."

She said, "*Abend*, Hans."

"*Abend*, Heather."

CHAPTER EIGHT
ECO VIN

Sleep did not come easily to Hans that night; he dreamed of castles and knights in battle, and then of lying next to his ladylove. He could feel the softness of her skin as his hand traced her curves. He awoke with a burning desire that he had not felt in such a long time. He got up and took a cold shower, and as the sun rose he took a walk, straight to Heather's pension.

***

Heather showered, put on her night top, and then adjusted the pillows so she could sit and read in bed. She was still impressed with how the beds were made up, large fluffed up pillows and then the bed cover filled with down. It was such a comfortable feeling. She pulled out the book entitled "*Südliche Weinstrasse*" the area in southwestern Germany along the wine route, and began to read:

"The love for wine in the southern Palatinate originated over 2000 years ago — the Romans felt right at home here. Richard the Lion-Hearted, on the other hand, had little opportunity for sensual pleasures during his stay at the Trifels imperial fortress during the 12th century; for it is here that he was incarcerated. During the last century, King Ludwig I of Bavaria came to this area of his own free will, however, and his Majesty immediately had the villa Ludwigshöhe built on the 'most beautiful square mile of the Reich.' The fortresses of Landeck, Madenburg,

Kropsburg, as well as a good dozen other bastions, are not simply mute monuments to history. They attract visitors today as well with their inns and taverns and the breathtaking view they provide over a sea of vineyards along the southern German wine route. If you pronounce the traditional toast 'to the health of the Palatinate' from this vantage point, you will literally find the Promised Land at your feet."

Heather stopped reading and tried to absorb what she had just learned. Here she was in the heart of a wine region, with ancient castles, each with a story to tell.

"How many stories were about love?" she wondered. Her thoughts quickly turned to the events that happened since she arrived: the touching of the stone, the flashback to another time, meeting Hans and realizing that they may have met in another lifetime. What would happen next? What mysteries awaited them?

"I must get that note translated," she said out loud. "I'm sure it will provide the key to the next step that must be taken."

***

Hans saw her walk down the stairs, wearing a lavender sweater and gray slacks. She looked radiant. He walked over to greet her.

"Good morning, Heather." He said.

"Good morning, Hans." She replied with a smile "Shall we have coffee?"

Heather was surprised when Hans suddenly announced, "Today you will get to taste an assortment of local wines and at the same time learn more about them. I have arranged with a *Weingut*—that is the German name for a producer of wines—to sample his wines."

"When? When can we do this?"

"Today. Right now if you like. The owner will be home all day."

"Good, let's do it. It sounds so exciting. Although I have had a number of different wines from America, I have also had some imports as well. This should be interesting."

"There is something else interesting with this particular wine grower. His wine is called *Eco Vin*. That means it is ecologically produced. He uses no unnatural chemical substances on his vineyards. All growing guidelines are ecologically sound. It also enhances the taste of the grape and, of course, the wine."

They proceeded to the *"Hohlreiter Weingut"* and were invited into the small *Weinstube* especially used for the tasting of wines. After introductions, the host reiterated what Hans had told her about the region and the methods they used in the production of their wines.

"I will do my best to explain things to you in English. But Herr Hess can help me out when I make a mistake. You have most likely heard about German white wines. Riesling is a popular German white wine in America. But what most Americans don't know is that we also have very good red wines. It is just a matter of time until this becomes more known. Most of the wines in this region are not blends, but consist of 100 percent of the grapes used in the wine. The name of the wine is the name of the grape and the vineyard where it is grown. For example, we'll start with a white wine – a Riesling. This is called Kaiserberg Riesling. It was grown in the vineyard named Kaiserberg."

He went on to discuss other wines such as Merlot, Dornfelder, Regent, Portugieser, Silvaner, Morio-Muskat, and

Kerner in their various forms. Each time a new wine was introduced, a small amount of wine was poured in a glass for each of them to taste. After tasting it and commenting on it, they ate a small piece of bread to remove the taste of the wine from their palates. In this manner, the tasting of the next wine would not be mingled with the previous one.

"There are no additives in our wine. Often people will complain of headaches from drinking certain wines, and it is most often due to substances added to enhance the taste. The cause of headaches can also be due to pesticides that find their way into the wine from spraying. Using additives is not the same as wine blending where a combination of wines are mixed to create an excellent tasting wine. And names are created for these wines to identify that particular blend. I would like to mention also that a well-designed and good-looking bottle does not mean it is a quality wine. "

Heather was enjoying herself learning about the wines of the region and also more about the quality of wines. At the same time, the consumption of the wine was beginning to have an affect on her. She was becoming very relaxed and in a dreamy mood. She knew she needed to get something in her stomach before she drank any more. She said, "Hans, I am starting to feel the effects of the wine, perhaps we should take a walk or have a meal."

The owner replied, "I may have just the solution. There is knoll just above the Kaiserberg vineyard. There is also a shade tree there." He grabbed a basket from under the tasking shelf and placed in it an assortment of *Käse*, *Brötchen* and *Wurst*. He then put a bottle of the Merlot in the basket and said, "Enjoy, the sun, the air and this beautiful day. The *Käse*, the *Wurst*, and the fine Merlot should help make it a pleasant experience." Then he winked at Hans.

Hans took the basket of cheese, hard rolls, sausage, and wine, got directions to the grassy knoll, and they started walking. As Heather felt the fresh air enter her lungs, she felt her head clear a little, but not as much as she would like. In a way, it was good feeling dreamy, although she had always been the type to be in control. Yet everything about this trip was out of control. Her feelings for Hans were definitely out of control. They walked through the vineyard and found the knoll. It had a beautiful view overlooking the rolling vineyards and the mountain range off to their right. There, sitting majestically as it had for hundreds of years, was the *Madenburg* castle. It somehow seemed fitting that they would have chosen this spot for a picnic.

Hans placed the basket under the tree and then spread the blanket that the wine owner had thoughtfully included. He opened the bottle of Merlot and said, "I need to let this breathe."

Then he laid out the spread of bread, cheese, and sausage. She thought of offering to help, but didn't want to interrupt Hans as he methodically went about carefully placing each item on the blanket. With a smile and bowing slightly, he said, "*Gnädiges Fraülein* (gracious lady), may I offer you some refreshments?"

"*Ja, mein Herr*," she said and quickly took a big chunk of bread with some cheese.

He smiled as she took a hasty bite of the hard bread.

"Are you making fun of me?"

Hans shook his head, "No, not at all. I just like the way you do things with enthusiasm."

"Is that a nice way of saying I am eating like a pig?"

He laughed, "Perhaps, but one with zest."

"I am just trying to get something in my stomach. I was starting to feel a bit dreamy with that wine."

"You know, it is okay to feel dreamy sometimes."

She shook her head smiling and said, "Maybe, but not for me."

She watched as Hans picked up the bottle of Merlot and poured a glass and handed it to her, then said, "Yes, even for you it is okay to feel dreamy."

She took the glass and holding it up said, "To your health, Hans."

He poured a glass and raised it to hers. "To your health, Heather."

They sipped their drink. Tasting the full body, the richness of the wine, she said, "This is a very nice Merlot."

"Yes, it is." They both took another sip.

As they were finishing their glass of wine, Heather said, "I almost forgot." She reached into her pocket and presented the note from the *Madenburg*.

He pulled out his reading glasses and unrolled the note. Holding it at a distance with his right arm, he said, "You know, you should be trying to translate this yourself, It is written in *Hochdeutsch, High German,* and that is what you are learning."

She moved closer to him and looked into his eyes and said, "You are right. Please teach me." Then she touched his left arm. She felt his response. He did not pull away, but rather she felt the hair on his arm stand on end, as goose bumps rose from his skin. She could have removed her hand, but she kept it on his arm for balance as she slightly leaned over him so she could better see the note. Her chest lightly touched his chest. She heard his breathing quicken, ever so slightly.

He cleared his throat, and said, "The first line reads. *'It was another weekend of wonder. What a joy to be alive. For I know I am in love,'* Yes, *'Liebe'* is *'love'*."

Heather responded, "*Liebe* is 'love'. I got it." She flashed him a smile.

Hans said, "Now, here in the second sentence, it says, 'Last night, My Champion and I danced during the ball, an entire dance just the two of us. I could see my father looking on as we danced. I hope that he sees what a good match we would be. Then this morning I received a note from My Champion asking me to join him on a picnic, just outside the castle. I knew I was taking a risk, but it was such a glorious day. He kissed me passionately, but as difficult as it was, I resisted him. I felt his desire for me grow as he talked of lovers for all time. Upon my return, I received a stern lecture from my mother for going out on a picnic. She spoke of bandits and wild animals, but I suspected she was more concerned about My Champion. Even her stern lecture could not dampen my joy as I think of My Champion as we go to the games in Bewartstein.'*

Heather sighed and said, "Young love."

Hans reached to hand her the note, and as he did so his hand inadvertently brushed ever so slightly across her breast. His hand stopped. She looked him in the eye, then down to his hand, and back to his eyes and smiled. Then she whispered, "Actually, it is more like new love, all the thrill of young love, with the knowledge from experience of how wonderful it can be."

His hand remained where it was against her breast. Heather looked up at him and whispered, "Like the excitement of a first kiss, knowing how wonderful it can feel." She leaned closer to him, their lips so close they could feel each other's breath. Then it happened. Their lips touched. She could feel the fullness of his mouth on hers, the taste of Merlot on his tongue, the way his kiss took her breath away, and she sensed it was the same for him. It was an exploratory kiss, one which grew quickly into a passionate kiss. They embraced as they kissed, and she could feel his chest against hers, their hearts beating in unison. She felt his hand exploring the softness of her breast outside her shirt. As they moved closer to one another, his hand guided her to lie down next to him. That was when she felt his growing desire as their kiss became more passionate. They broke from the kiss and looked into each other's eyes.

She whispered, "Wow. That was some first kiss."

"Yes. Yes, it was."

She sat upright and said, "So the next castle is *Bewartstein*."

"Yes, *Bewartstein*."

She looked at the bottle of Merlot and said, "That was some very good wine. I think I will get me some. Right now, though, I think we should be heading back."

They gathered their things and put them in the basket. Finally they both stood and walked down to the winery. Thanking the winery owner for the tasting and the picnic basket, they departed.

They drove back in silence. Heather had never felt a kiss like that one before. Compassion, passion, and desire all rolled into one. Her mind was still spinning. She gave Hans a quick peck on the check as he dropped her off at her pension.

Sleep was difficult for Hans. He dreamed of castles and knights in battle, and then of lying next to his ladylove. He could feel the softness of her skin as his hand traced her curves. He awoke with a burning desire that was becoming more frequent. He got up and took another cold shower.

***

Hans was beginning to think more and more about his relationship with Heather. That kiss was much more than he had expected. He was becoming very attached to her and knew where it could lead, if he let it. But he couldn't let it; he was married. It had not been a marriage in the true sense for many years, even before the coma. Since then, many had urged him to get on with his life. If this relationship with Heather went further, was he man enough to make her happy? The difference in age was a factor to consider. What if he couldn't satisfy her as a man? That would not only be unfair to her and a huge disappointment, but it would also be devastating to his ego. Although his sexual urges were very strong at times, as he felt when they kissed, could they be sustained? Desire and capability were certainly separate things. He realized the difference in age and wondered if he was doing the right thing. Of course, he had heard about new products to assist in that regard, but he had never had the need even to try them. Absence of sexual activity was not because he had been incapable, but because his wife was incapacitated. He had tried and succeeded in suppressing those urges rather than looking for someone just to quell his sexual desires.

He realized that he must stop thinking and dreaming about Heather. It would be better to become more distant. Perhaps he should decline to assist her on this quest of finding the notes. The notes were about another time in the past. Who were they kidding to think that there was an association with the present?

That night Hans had dreams, vivid dreams, not like before where it was hard to tell if it was he or some knight from the past. This time it was he, and Heather, and they kissed, gently and deeply. In his dream, he could taste the Merlot on her lips, the sweetness of her breath, and the softness of her lips. His hand caressed her breast, feeling the fullness and softness of her skin. She broke from the kiss and looked him straight in the eye. Then she began to unbutton her blouse. He took a deep breath. She took much time with each button, each time exposing more creamy white skin. His hands explored the newly exposed skin, and she smiled approvingly. Finally he took her shirt off, exposing her deep plunging light pink bra.

She looked at him with a smile and then undid the front snap on her bra. His eyes grew wide at the fullness of her breasts, the soft skin, and the dark nipples. His hands couldn't resist, and she looked at him with that approving smile. As he touched her, his alarm clock went off. He was feeling the desire in a way that was hard to subdue. There was a throbbing in his loins, a stiffness that he had not felt in a long while. Last night he needed two glasses of wine to calm down before retiring. He couldn't start drinking this early in the morning. How could he be having these urges at his age? It had to stop!

Yes, it must be stopped! It has already gone too far. I must discourage her from seeking my help.

Hans sat down and crafted a note.

Ms. Wilson,

Although I had promised my nephew that I would be your guide, I feel that I can no longer provide that service. I believe that you have acquired some romantic notions of knights and castles and place me in some sort of leading role. Admittedly the notion of a beautiful, younger woman showing romantic intentions has warmed my heart, and I may have for a moment been swept up in the drama of it all, but the kiss last night brought me to my senses. And for that reason I must discontinue my services.

Hans Hess

Hans took the note to the pension early in the morning, and left it with the front desk. He had to force himself to walk away. He thought he might just watch her to make sure she got the note. No, he could not. He couldn't watch her heart break, which was exactly what it was going to do. He knew it, but he knew it was for the best.

He walked back to his house, pulled out the note wrapped in the cloth, and unrolled it. It had the exact same handwriting as the two notes he had deciphered, the same type of paper, the same quality of ink. He read the first sentence of the note.

"I close these notes that tell a tale of a great love and sorrow. He was willing to give his life for my love, and I gave my love for his life. The notes have been hidden in the Castles where we danced, loved and lost. They can only be found by those who are truly in love, soul mates, that will feel our love and loss as if it were their own, until someday our souls can be united as one. Whoever possesses this note must now seek the next note. The chain cannot be broken without harm befalling the holder of this note. The first note of our love can be found in the Castle Landeck."

This was the note that he found in the Castle at *Trifels* almost 30 years ago when he was stationed in Germany. He had held onto it all this time. It was the note that brought him back to this same region. He had taken his wife to the castle many times, hoping that together they would find the first note, the first clue. He had given up hope when she fell ill, but still he was drawn to the castle.

When Heather found the note, he realized it was she, and not he, who was destined to find the notes. In a way, he was flattered when she shared the note with him. He thought it might actually be his destiny, too. But whom was he kidding?

***

Heather woke with such renewed energy and spirit. Who would have thought she would have come all the way to Germany to find a man as wonderful as Hans. She knew he was older, but that didn't matter to her. In fact, if anything, it was his age, his wisdom, his patience, his understanding that made him even more appealing. And the kiss last night had sent chills through her in a way she had not felt in a long, long time. She couldn't wait to see him today, to hear his voice, touch his arm, and perhaps even get another kiss.

She showered and quickly dressed. There was a part of her that wanted to call him, find out what time they would get together. But he was always there, or at the very least he would leave a note. She bounced down the stairs in anticipation of the day, a smile on her face and love on her mind. She poured herself some coffee, had a muffin, and sat down in the window seat where she would have a clear view of the direction from which he always came. She was basking in the sun when the owner of the pension placed the note on her table.

"*Danke Schön,*" she thanked him.

Heather suspected that Hans had been called away on business again, and hence the purpose of the note. She opened and read it. His words cut through her like a knife. If he meant to hurt her, he had done a good job of it. She had pushed for the kiss and scared him off. She was angry with herself. She should have known better. She went back to her room, trying to figure out what to do next.

She looked at the books she had purchased. It was time she learned to take care of herself. Without Hans around to guide her, she would need to learn the language. She took the tape, put it in a tape player, and read along with the book. She spent most of the day in her room, going through her tape and book. It helped to keep her mind focused on something, anything, to keep her mind off Hans.

Yet during the day she thought of him. She wondered what he was thinking, what he was doing. Why did she care if he had dumped her? No. the truth was, he had been dignified, and she had stepped over the line and he finally put an end to her silliness.

She had a restless night, dreaming of knights and maidens and of Hans' kiss. She was angry with herself thinking of him again. Perhaps it was the unsolved mystery of the notes. She decided that the next day she would take a trip to *Bewartstein*, in search of the next note. She was sure that once she found it she would be able to get these thoughts out of her mind. She could do this without Hans Hess.

That night she pulled out a map and traced her route to the castle. Then she pulled out her books about the castle. Again her night was restless with dreams that didn't make any sense.

She woke early the next morning for her trip. She drove in the direction of the village, Hauenstein, and then turned toward Vorderweidenthal. It was only a short distance from there to Erlenbach, where *Burg Bewartstein* was located. Heather picked up her book of information and read:

> "The first documentary reference to the castle dates from 1152. In 1314 Strasbourg and Hagenau, two cities of the Holy Roman Empire, besieged the castle and destroyed large parts of the construction after they won the castle. In 1480 Bewartstein became the property of Hans von Trotha, who reinforced the mediaeval structure and the isolated gun turret on the mountain of Nestelberg. Considerably damaged by a fire at the beginning of the 17th century, the castle remained a ruin for nearly 300 years. Its current appearance dates back to the reconstruction of Theodor Hoffmann, called von Baginsky, at the end of the 19th century."

Heather toured the castle; it was large and so intact that there was so much to see. She was able to read some of the signs as a result of her hours of study, but she missed Hans so much. She searched rooms, looking for a guest room where a window might be. Both the previous notes had been hidden in a spot that allowed her to look out the window. However, this castle was so large and there were so many rooms and chambers, many of which were not accessible. Her first day in search of a note was unsuccessful.

She decided to get a room at a pension below in the village of Erlenbach and come back the next day in search of the note. As she wandered through the castle, she came across the lower levels, dungeons where torture chambers were still preserved intact with equipment. It gave her the chills to think of what had taken place there.

After three days of searching the castle she knew she was missing something—a key of sorts to finding the next message. The only thing she could do was to go back to the *Madenburg* and *Landeck* castles, hoping to put together some type of clue. Why she needed to find the next note, she didn't know, but somehow it possessed her thoughts. Thoughts in which Hans Hess appeared.

The next day she made her way to the *Madenburg*. She went to the very spot where she found the note, took out her sketchpad, and quickly sketched the chamber. Then she sketched the chamber in relation to the castle itself, hoping that she could make some sense of the notes and their location from her sketches.

As she was leaving, she went back to the column where she and Hans had touched and both saw the young couple dancing. She was sure of the column; it was in the middle of the room. She felt nothing. She saw no visions of a young couple. Absolutely no sensation whatsoever. Then she tried every column in the room, and still felt nothing.

On her drive back to Klingenmünster she stopped at the spot where they had a picnic. She touched the old stone, and once again felt nothing. Maybe it was just a temporary moment of insanity. But tomorrow she would retrace her steps to *Burg Landeck*.

She stayed that night at the same pension she had previously stayed at in Göcklingen, and the next morning hiked to *Landeck* on the trail that Hans had shown her. She had her sketchpad and camera with her as she hiked the hill. Finally she made it to the top and went immediately to the archway, where she first felt the strong visions with Hans. She touched the stone, waiting for something, anything, and there was nothing. She mumbled and then went out in the courtyard, where she had the vision of dancers in a Quadrille. She felt nothing. She saw no visions. Finally she went back to the chamber where she found the note. She sat on the bench and sketched the chamber and then the chamber's position within the castle.

Frustrated more than anything, she headed down the trail to town and her pension. She was in a hurry and the slope was steep. Not paying attention to where she stepped, she tripped over a protruding root. Her sketchpad went flying in one direction, and she in the other. She was tumbling down the side of the mountain on a slippery surface, sliding toward the edge of a steep cliff. She tried grabbing hold of some tree limbs to stop her rapid descent, and just as she was about to go over the edge, she managed to grasp a limb and wrap her leg around it. The limb bent sharply from her weight, leaving her hanging over the cliff.

CHAPTER NINE
THE RESCUE

Hans had not seen or heard from Heather since he left his note. It had been five days already and he longed to see her again. This wasn't supposed to be this difficult. He learned that she had checked out of her pension the day after he left her the note. His life was once again boring, without meaning, still hopefully waiting for the eventuality of his wife's recovery.

Hans returned to his daily routine, daily hikes into the forest and up the steep trail to *Burg Landeck*. He had things to do in town, helping out neighbors, or running errands, and today he got a late start for his walk. He almost considered canceling it, but then decided he must complete his agenda – regardless. As he hiked up the trail toward *Landeck,* he spied a piece of a paper. He picked it up and found a sketch, a beautiful, almost professional looking sketch of the *Landeck* castle layout. Then he saw another piece of paper, another sketch of *Landeck*, of a chamber within the castle. He had been in this chamber numerous times. As he continued on his way he found yet another sketch. He looked at it and immediately recognized the layout of the *Madenburg*. It was too much of a coincidence. He spied another sketch of a chamber in the *Madenburg*, the chamber where they had found the note.

He knew by the quality of the sketches, the subject matter, that only one person could have drawn them. He shouted, "Heather, are you here?"

He looked at the sketches again, and panic struck him. She would never let these sketches just litter the trail. Something was wrong, something was seriously wrong. He shouted again, "Heather, are you here?"

He listened and then shouted, "Heather, where are you?"

He then heard a faint sound, coming from the side of the mountain. He rushed towards the sound and the edge of the trail.

He looked over the edge and saw her. Or at least he thought it was she, hanging on a tree limb protruding over the edge of the cliff. He shouted, "Heather."

Then he heard her shout, "Here! I'm over here!"

He rushed down the hill. Sure enough, she was clinging to the branch as though perched on it. He saw her face, her hands, and her clothes. It was obvious she had taken a fall, narrowly escaping a fatal plunge. As he looked at her hanging there, his mind was filled with questions of how or where to start. Trying to use some levity to ease her mind, he said, "I'll bet the view is pretty good from there?"

She looked at him and was not amused. "I'm hanging on a tree limb sticking out over a cliff, one wrong move and I am gone, and you are asking me about the view?"

He started laughing and then she started laughing.

He said, "I would ask how you got there, but I think it's pretty obvious."

"Nothing gets past you, does it Hans?" she said sarcastically. "Now, if you would be so kind as to use that brilliant mind of yours to figure out a way to get me away from here."

Hans continued to evaluate the situation. *This is going to be tricky*, he thought.

When Hans took his hikes he routinely carried a small backpack. In it was a bottle of water that he always placed in fresh. There was also a small first aid kit, some toilet tissue, and a hunting knife. It wasn't much, but it was all he had to work with.

He quickly removed his backpack and extended the straps to full length. It was not enough. He needed at least three feet beyond the length of his arm to reach Heather.

He took the knife and cut the straps from the backpack. Then he tied them together, extending the length, and finally took off his belt, hoping it would give him the length he needed.

Heather observed Hans as he worked. He worked swiftly and yet kept up a light chatter as he did so, attempting to divert her attention from her precarious perch. She was in great danger and it wouldn't help matters for her to panic. He would need her help, and it was important that she remain calm. He noted that the limb wouldn't hold much longer as the roots had pulled away, first when she grabbed it and now that her weight was causing the roots to loosen their hold. He fought off the anxiety he was experiencing. *What if I should lose her?* At that moment he felt the strongest attachment to her, as though she were already a part of him. Now he blamed himself. If he had not written the note she would have been safe with him. Had he driven her here? *It is all my fault. I must save her. I must!*

Hans approached her position cautiously.

"My dear, just be patient and let this old geezer pull you off that silly perch." Despite herself, Heather couldn't help but smile.

"I will throw the end of the strap to you. Try to catch it with your one hand. When you do, wrap it around your wrist through that small loop so you have a good grip, Okay?"

"Okay, Hans. Just get me out of here!"

Hans threw the strap to her and she tried to grasp it, but missed. Her movement caused some of the ground surrounding the roots to give way, and the limb moved downward several inches. Heather stifled a scream. She was perspiring and her face had lost its color. Hans realized that the small downward movement would make it even more difficult for her to reach the strap now. He was dealing with precious inches with the length of the strap and couldn't afford to lose any more.

Heather remained very quiet, but her grip had tightened around the limb. It would be difficult for her to release that grip to make a second attempt at grasping the strap when Hans threw it.

"You almost had it, Heather. It was my fault. I will throw it more to your right so that it will be over the center of the limb. Are you ready?"

Heather didn't reply, but nodded. Hans carefully swung the strap back and forth to get the right angle and then said, "Here it comes!"

Heather reached and grabbed it, holding on tightly. It was not a good enough grip to pull her up yet, and she needed to work slowly with just one hand to improve her hold. Carefully, with Hans advising her, she had the strap firmly in her grasp and said, "Please, Hans, get me out of here."

Hans began to pull her toward him. As each small tug inched her toward him it also caused more ground to give way. The limb kept moving downward.

"Okay! This is it, Heather! With the next pull I want you to release your hand from the limb so I can pull you up over the edge. Are you ready?"

She nodded. Hans gave a big heave and she released her grip of the limb at the same time. Momentarily she swung free over the precipice until Hans grabbed her arm and pulled her over the top and away from the edge.

Heather stayed where she lay, completely exhausted. A tear appeared in the corner of one eye and then tears from both eyes began to flow as she sobbed softly.

Hans lay next to her, wrapping his arm around her. He fought back his own emotions at the relief he felt that she was safe.

He saw a long scrap on her leg that was bleeding. Her arm had another scrape, as did her face, and then he saw a lot of blood on her shirt. He said, "You have some bad cuts there. Let me fix them."

He moved her farther away from the cliff and grabbed the first aid kit. He looked at the cut on her arm first and said, "This is going to sting a bit," as he cleaned out the wound with alcohol. Then he gently rubbed on some antibiotic cream and placed a large band-aide over the cut.

He smiled at her and said, "Now, was that so bad?"

Through her tear-stained face, she smiled and said, "No. It wasn't."

Then he looked after the cut on her cheek, and cleaned it with a swab. Their eyes met and she said, "Thank you."

"You really should have yourself checked out. By the look of these cuts, you took a pretty good fall. Do you have pain anywhere?"

"I'll be okay."

"Would you cooperate with me, your temporary doctor?"

"What do you want me to do?"

"Bend your legs one at a time. First the left. Good. And now the right. Good. Any pain?" She shook her head.

"Please do the same with your arms. Right one. Good. Now the left one. Any pain?" Again she shook her head.

"Okay. One final thing: I want you to pull your knees up to your chest. Do it slowly. If you experience any pain, stop at once."

Heather did as requested and slowly pulled her legs up and then back down again without any indication of pain.

He put some antibiotic cream on the cut on her cheek and then a band-aide. He smiled and she smiled, and then he said, "Good as new."

He looked at the cut on her leg. She had a pair of khaki slacks and the cut on her leg had ripped the pant leg along the thigh. He said, "It is hard to see how bad that cut on your leg is."

Heather looked at the rip and the blood around the cut, and ripped the pant leg a little more, along the cut and said, "There, is that enough, to see the cut?" Hans was surprised by her action. She must have read his expression, because she said, "Look, the pants are already ruined."

She lay on her side, allowing the cut to face upward. Hans observed her long legs and her hips curving from her narrow waist. Her leg was now partially exposed along the newly ripped section of slacks. He needed to focus. He gently pulled the material away and cleansed the wound. There was a softness to her skin that he noticed as he worked. He put some antibiotic cream on the long cut and then fashioned a bandage out of gauze that he cut into strips.

He looked at her, assessing her injuries. All her major cuts were bandaged except for one, and he also saw a decent amount of blood on the side of her shirt.

"It looks like you have a pretty good cut on your side under your shirt.

She looked. "Is my shirt torn?"

"It doesn't appear to be."

Almost as surprising as her ripping her pant leg, she unbuttoned her shirt and took it off. Hans couldn't help but stare at the light pink lace bra with noticeable cleavage.

"Don't tell me you haven't been to the beach before. This bra provides a lot more coverage than many bathing suits. Besides, this is a $50 tailor made shirt for my long arms. I am not about to rip it up."

At the sight of the pink bra, Hans experienced an immediate flashback to his dream. He saw himself opening the front of the bra, feeling those wonderfully shaped breasts, running his fingers over the nipples that became firm and inviting, just waiting to be….

"Hans! Is there something wrong? You look flushed."

Hans quickly turned aside so she could not see below his waist and the effect she was having on him. "No, nothing's wrong. I was just giving some thought to that cut," he lied.

The cut had opened up pretty bad. It was on her side between her hip and half way up her rib cage. He asked her to lie on her side. She complied. Hans looked at the cut, but every now and then he looked at her cleavage, now exaggerated by the way she lay. He shook himself so that he could concentrate on what he was doing. The cut wasn't as deep as it had appeared to be, and he was able to clean it easily. It would have been done a lot sooner if he had not been so distracted. After he had finished with the bandaging, she put her shirt back on and said with a grin, "So is that it, or have you found cuts in other embarrassing places?"

Hans smiled, and said, "No, but I would feel better if you would see a doctor."

"That's okay, you did a great job."

She slowly stood up and said, "Well, I guess I better be on my way before I make too big a fool of myself."

"A little late for that, isn't it?"

"Thanks. I mean that sincerely. Thanks for everything, Hans." She turned and started up the hill.

"The sketches, the sketches on the trail, you drew those didn't you?"

Heather turned around and said, "Yes. Why?"

"They are very good sketches of the *Landeck* and the *Madenburg*."

"I am an architect, you know. That is what I do. I draw sketches of buildings and rooms inside of buildings."

He could tell by the briskness of her tone that she was trying to salvage what little pride she had. He asked, "Why did you draw them?"

"Because they were there." She was almost to the top of the hill and the trail, and he rushed to catch up to her.

"They were individual sketches of the chambers where you found the notes. You are trying to figure out where the note is hidden in *Burg Bewartstein*, aren't you? That is an ingenious idea."

Heather stared at him with an anger that boiled just below the surface and replied, "I was planning to use the sketches, but not anymore."

"Why not? It is a good idea."

"I went to *Burg Bewartstein* to search for the note. I couldn't find it. End of story."

The warning on his note flashed through his mind. "But the sketches. You came back, looking for clues."

"It is silly. I just got caught up in the silly romance of those notes and embarrassed myself by coming on to you. It is time I went back home and faced life."

"When did you decide to give up the quest for the notes?"

"As I was coming down the hill today I reminded myself that I am a partner in a major firm and here I am looking for mysterious notes. For what reason?"

Hans whispered, "Right before the fall."

Heather replied, "Yeah, right before the fall."

"You can't give up on your quest for the notes."

Heather, now reaching the top of the hill, started down the other side with Hans right behind her, repeating what he had said. "You can't give up on the quest."

She stopped, turned to him and said, "Why are you doing this to me? You made it clear in your note that this was a silly idea."

"You aren't telling me everything, Heather. It is more than my note. You went to *Burg Bewartstein* in search of the notes after receiving my note."

She stared at him and said, "Okay, you want to know the truth? It's not there. The feeling, the visions, they're gone. They are gone at *Landeck*. They are gone at *Madenburg*, and they are even gone from the picnic area near *Madenburg*. There is no reason to continue."

Suddenly the note Hans possessed began to make much more sense. She found the note after they met, after they touched the wall. It wasn't just Heather's quest, it was their quest, but her life was the one at risk if they didn't continue the quest, since she possessed the notes.

"I won't let you give up the quest."

Heather turned again facing him, her eyes full of anger. She said, "You won't let me give up the quest? Exactly who do you think you are?"

"Your tutor, your guide. You came here to learn the mystery of the castles. Grab your sketches, and we will go down to town and tomorrow we will plan our trip to *Burg Bewartstein*." Hans looked at her. Could he sway her over with the half-truth? Could he go on this quest and not reveal his feelings towards her? He must.

She looked at him thoughtfully. She saw his handsome face and the pleading in his eyes, and then said, "Okay, okay, let's do it."

ABE F. MARCH

CHAPTER TEN
THE HIKE TO *BEWARTSTEIN*

Heather woke feeling the bruises from her fall. She hadn't taken a fall like that since she was in college playing volleyball. She was stiff and could feel the tightness in her arms and legs from holding onto the limb for as long as she did. As she sat commiserating about her aches, she realized how age was creeping up on her. She also knew how lucky she was that Hans came along when he did.

Her thoughts flashed to Hans. He was the most complicated man she had known in a long time. Actually, that was the point. She really didn't know him. One day she gets a note saying that her quest for the notes is a fanciful fantasy and that he will have no part of it, and then a few days later he is insisting that she continue the quest with an urgency that almost seemed like a matter of life and death. He was holding something back from her. She was convinced of it. She had not succeeded in business without being able to read people. Hans Hess was keeping a secret from her, and before this trip was over she would know that secret.

The other thing she was sure of was that Hans was attracted to her, and yet he was hiding his feelings, perhaps even from himself. She had sensed for a long time that he had a sexual attraction towards her; of course, the feeling was mutual. But after getting his note, she wasn't sure; maybe it was just wishful thinking. When he had been so kind and caring, mending her cuts and scraps, she decided she had to know if there was something there. When she took her shirt off, she knew for sure. His eyes, his flushed face gave him away. The fact was, she was glad he was going to be her guide again. She missed him dearly. Perhaps she should have played harder to convince, pushed him to admit he liked her, and pushed him to share his secret. No, she was getting exactly what she wanted, Hans in her life again. With the quest for the notes revitalized, she could wait for another time to learn his secrets, when he was ready to reveal them.

She went to her desk drawer and pulled out her sketches. She looked at the rooms and the relationship to the room and the castle to see if there were any similarities. Both rooms were in a tower of sorts, both on the upper floors, both rooms had windows, and both notes were found in the grout under the bench. However, there were differences, as well. The rooms were in different corners of the castle. "How will I ever find the right room at *Burg Bewartstein*?" she wondered. There were so many possibilities to explore.

She looked at the map in her book on castles. *Burg Bewartstein* was located about 25 kilometers from the other two castles by roads. She looked at the location of *Landeck* and *Madenburg*. She took her sketches and placed them on the map, at the correct orientation. She penciled in a line looking out from the window at *Landeck,* another line looking out from the window of *Madenburg*, the two lines intersected. She sketched a line from where the two points intersected back to *Burg Bewartstein*. She pulled out a detailed map. There was a tower. She circled the tower in pencil, and decided that would be where she would begin her search. Now she couldn't wait to get started.

***

Hans walked directly to the *Pfalzklinik* care facility. Nurse Gretchen, as usual, was at the front window. When she saw Herr Hess she anticipated his question: *"Ist sie schon wach?"*

"Noch nicht, Herr Hess," she said as she buzzed the door.

"Danke, Gretchen."

He walked directly to Monica's room and watched her briefly from the doorway. Monica lay as usual, appearing to be in a deep sleep. He entered the room, sat on the edge of her bed and said, "My dear, I will be going away again. It is important for me to look for the notes. Tonight I realized that the warning in the note I hold is real. I tried to turn my back on the note, but now I worry that I could cost a woman her life. I must go on this quest. My dear, I am concerned that this quest may take me from you in more ways than one." He paused and then said, "Who am I kidding? You have been gone from me for a long time, even before you came here." He stood up and said, "I do love you, but it is time for me to go."

As he left the clinic, he said, "Gretchen, I will be away for a few days. If anything happens please call me at this number." He handed her his pager number.

Hans decided that it might help matters if they were to hike rather than drive. He would wait until the morning to make sure that Heather had recovered from the fall. In the meanwhile, he would prepare two backpacks with enough provisions to get them to *Burg Bewartstein* in a leisurely fashion. He liked being prepared. If there were no accommodations available at the castle or in the village, he was equipped to camp out. It would be a slow fifteen to twenty kilometer hike through the forest, and he wanted to be ready for any eventuality.

It was now becoming a mission; one that must be completed or something terrible would befall one or both of them. He was a man of the world who didn't believe in fate or in magic, but what he had experienced at the castle, being catapulted back in time, had changed his mind. There was an unknown power involved with the notes and he knew that he must complete the mission.

He carefully mapped out the route. Just before reaching the castle, they would cross a stream, the Wieslauter. He smiled to himself, thinking about the story he would tell her about this stream and the knight who lived in the castle. The antics of the knight always amused him.

He made a final review of the planned route. They would set out from the *Landeck* Castle and make their way to Liebfrauenberg. From there they would go to Birkenhördt, on to Lauterschwan, and then to Erlenbach. *Bewartstein* stood on the hill directly above Erlenbach.

He had left a note for Heather informing her that they would be hiking to *Bewartstein*, if she was up to it, and to dress appropriately.

Heather was prompt. She came down the stairs wearing a loose fitting shirt and comfortable looking three quarter length khaki pants. He was surprised to see that she also wore hiking shoes. She carried a jacket over her shoulder and a large handbag. He assumed she carried her personal and feminine articles in that.

"*Morgen*, Heather."

"*Morgen*, Hans. Looks like you've got everything packed and ready to go."

"I hope I have everything we'll need. It seems no matter how carefully one plans, there is always something forgotten. You are suitably dressed for a hike. Did you bring hiking clothes with you or were they purchased locally?"

"I bought them in Landau last week. You approve?" she said with a smile.

"Yes. You look lov…" He cleared his throat and said, "You are suitably dressed, as I mentioned. And I compliment you on your purchase. Do you feel up to it?"

"Yes, I feel just fine."

"Good. Shall we go?"

"I'm ready. Is there room for my hand bag in the backpack?"

"I think we can fit it in."

After tugging and stuffing, the bag was closed. "I trust it is not too heavy. I can't get any more into mine. You will let me know when you need a rest, won't you?"

Heather had an amused look on her face, but didn't say anything, and Hans immediately knew that she would try to show him how capable she really was. She handled the backpack easily and adjusted the straps comfortably.

"I know this may sound funny, but can we just hike anywhere we please without trespassing?"

"Actually, yes. When I first got here it was one of the things that gave me such a sense of freedom. The freedom to walk most anywhere one pleases without being stopped by some 'No Trespassing' sign. I don't recall ever seeing a sign that forbids access."

"Is it all public land, then?"

"Oh, not at all. Much of the forest is publicly owned, but even where there is private ownership there is nothing forbidding access. I think what is misleading is the absence of homes spread throughout the countryside. Even though one owns a bit of property in the forest doesn't mean he can build on it. They use it primarily for harvesting wood. As I may have mentioned before, building is restricted to areas designated for building and where services are provided."

"That is so different from where I live. One can only hike in public places such as parks, and even in those places there are so many rules."

"There are rules here, too, but most are common sense rules. You are supposed to stay on the designated paths so as not to disturb the wildlife. And when it is very dry, smoking in the forest is forbidden. I like to explore. There are many unusual rock formations here in the *Pfälzerwald,* and when I come across one that looks interesting, I like to check it out. I have found many places where people hid or found shelter during the war. That fascinates me. And there is still evidence of foxholes and trenches used during the war. Most of the bunkers have been blown up and covered over, but there are still some around."

"That sounds so exciting. Will you show me some?"

"Yes, but I think we should stay focused on the castles at the moment."

Heather laughed and said, "Yes, you're right, of course. It seems that I want to see everything at once."

They began their trek toward *Landeck.* Hans was relieved that he had caught himself before he said "lovely" in describing her appearance. He was determined to control his emotions and not let his feelings show. When they reached the castle, they stopped for a drink of water, but did not enter. Heather was looking at the bridge to the castle where she had first glimpsed Hans when she arrived here. She glanced at Hans now, but remained silent.

On impulse she said, "Hans, come here please." Hans followed her as she walked to the arch where they both saw the first vision. She took his hand and together they touched the arch, as they had done that first day. The vision of the young couple's first kiss flooded their minds. Her eyes locked onto his, she smiled and said, "The visions are back. You are part of the mystery of the notes, Hans, like it or not."

Hans nodded and said, "Yes, I know. That is why I insisted that you continue your quest."

Hans began walking and Heather followed. It was a new direction for Heather, and she followed him almost in a step-for-step fashion. At some places, they could walk side by side, and at others single file became necessary. They discussed the variety of trees and compared them to similar trees in America. There were also the numerous interesting red sandstone rock formations along the way that would normally have Hans investigating, but not today. The chatter of birds seemed to acknowledge their presence, and Heather would occasionally stop to listen to the strange new sounds.

They started up a steep incline, and Heather scurried ahead of Hans. As she picked her way ahead of him, he couldn't help but notice her firm buttocks and powerful legs. She moved along with ease, and Hans tried his best not to show any fatigue as he tried to keep pace with her. He was not about to give her a reason to gloat. As they continued, he remembered seeing a similar scene in a magazine years ago. It was a picture taken in the Amazon where a very attractive, but solidly built woman was leading a group of adventurers through the jungle. *Amazon lady,* thought Hans. *Perhaps I should find a nickname for her,* he thought with amusement.

They came to a clearing and Hans suggested they take a short break. He noted that she was perspiring, but showed no signs of being tired. *It could be a front of some sort,* thought Hans. But he had to admit to himself that she was a very agile and very tough lady.

Heather sat down on some soft leaves surrounded by moss and stretched her long legs out in front of her. "What kinds of animals are there in these parts? Are there snakes?"

"No. No snakes." Hans said emphatically. "That's one of the reason I enjoy hiking in this country. No poisonous snakes. The only thing that even resembles a snake is a very large snake-like worm. It is blind and harmless. It's called a *Blindschleiche*."

"Hans. I'm surprised. You're afraid of snakes?" she said with a grin.

"Yes, I will admit that I am."

"But why? Certainly you can determine the poisonous from the harmless."

"I suppose it has much to do with an experience I had as a kid. Where we lived there were copperheads and rattlers. Occasionally people were bitten and some died. But that's not what caused my deep fear of them. It had to do with some Evangelist that came to our church and associated the snake with evil and the devil. The lady Evangelist told a story about a snake that was trying to attack her because she represented good. And I could never get the picture she painted, of the snake coming after her, out of my mind. I used to dream of snakes chasing me."

"That's horrible! How could anyone do such a thing?"

"Yes, it was a horrible thing to say in the presence of an impressionable young child. But the whole theme in those days was creating fear of the devil to drive people to God. I don't like to associate fear with God. I like to think of a God of Love."

"Yes, me, too. Love in all its forms is good. Don't you think so Hans?"

Just the word, love, in the presence of Heather made his heart beat faster. He needed to change the subject quickly.

"Yes, I think so too. And I think we need to be on our way," he said rising and reaching for his backpack.

They made good progress and stopped for a picnic lunch. It was pleasant to sit alone in the forest with Heather and enjoy the quietness of their surroundings. Having her here with him felt so natural. There was little conversation as each seemed to be deep in thought. He wondered what she was thinking. He also wondered what events lay ahead that could affect their relationship and perhaps their life.

They stopped to observe some deer that stood watching them with their ears perked, ready for flight at the slightest movement in their direction.

"These deer are called *Reh*. They are small compared to the deer in the south of the country where the larger deer, called *Hirsch*, are more prevalent."

"Do you hunt, Hans?"

"No. I gave up my guns when I left America and have no ambition to kill anything. Here guns are not permitted unless for good reason, such as hunting. And hunting is strictly controlled. Anyone who wishes to hunt joins a hunting club. They must go through a course of study to qualify and then hunt only when and where designated. Usually the hunters belong to the club for the social aspect. After a hunt, there is a big feast and lots of drink to celebrate their success."

"What animal made all this mess?" Heather said pointing to an area where the earth was rooted up leaving noticeable evidence of forage.

"*Wildschweine*. Wild pigs did that. The forests in this area are full of *Kastanien Bäume* – Chestnut trees. People come from long distances in the fall of the year just to gather chestnuts. Of course, there's plenty remaining on the ground and it provides a source of food for the *Wildschweine.*"

"I often hear of wild boars attacking people. Do you think we will see any?"

Hans chuckled and said, "I doubt it. They are frightened of people and stay hidden. They do most of their hunting for food during the night and it is rare to see them during the day."

Heather was enjoying herself. She was alone in the forest with Hans, who she knew was becoming more and more a part of her life. She was learning new things about the country and expanding her vocabulary at the same time. What a wonderful feeling she had. She watched as Hans picked his way carefully along the path, stepping over the gnarled roots and protruding stones. It would be easy to overturn an ankle; he was obviously an experienced hiker. Every now and then he would turn to look back to see that she was keeping up and was all right, but he need not have worried about her keeping up. She was always close on his heels, seemingly pushing him forward. Her youth in comparison to his age was becoming more evident as they progressed.

It was in the late afternoon when they reached the stream in the valley below the castle. The *Bewartstein* Castle could be seen in the distance. Excitement showed on Heather's face as she took in the view.

"What's the name of this stream?"

"The Wieslauter. It does have an interesting story attached to it involving the Knight of *Bewartstein*. Would you like to hear it?"

"Yes, please."

"The knight lived here from 1467 to 1503. His name was *Hans von Trotha,* and came to be called Hans Trapp. He had a continuing quarrel with the bishop from the monastery in Weissenburg. Weissenburg is just over the border in France where this stream flows, and the monastery is situated directly on the Wieslauter. Anyway, the bishop wanted possession of the castle and the knight refused. This quarrel kept going for years. To aggravate the bishop, the knight would dam up the

Wieslauter, cutting off their supply of water, and then when the water was high enough, he would release the water and it would flood the monastery. The Bishop worked to have him excommunicated from the Catholic Church and succeeded. Yet when he died, he had managed things so that he would be buried in the church. His bones rest at the small St. Anna Chapel below the castle near here. We'll be able to see it from the castle and we can also go there later if you wish."

"That would be nice. I like to hear about characters like that, people who were not intimidated by the church."

They stood by the stream watching the water make its way around and over rocks causing ripples as it went. Hans sat down and started taking off his shoes.

"This is a good place to cool off. Do you want to join me?"

Heather sat down and quickly took off her shoes. She rolled up the legs of her pants and without a word dashed ahead of Hans into the water.

"Oooooh, the water is cold," she exclaimed, "but very refreshing."

"Be careful Heather. Those rocks are …."

He never got the word "slippery" out of his mouth as she plunged into the stream. Hans jumped in after her, but before he reached her, she stood up laughing hysterically. Hans reached for her hand, and she grabbed his hand and pulled. He lost his balance and plunged into the water. When he came up she was still laughing and he broke out laughing with her. When they stopped and looked at each other, it became even funnier, but a bit embarrassing for Hans. Heather's clothes clung to her, revealing every curve on her body. The nipples of her beautiful breasts protruded through her shirt as though she was wearing nothing underneath. Heather looked down at herself and quickly placed her hands over her breasts and then changed her mind and placed her hands down by her side. She continued to look Hans in the eyes as he tried to regain his composure.

"We've got to get out of these wet clothes quickly. It will be cooling down soon and by then we need to be dry."

"What do you mean, get out of these clothes?"

"I mean exactly that. We can't show up at the castle, or anywhere else, for that matter, soaking wet. You do have other clothes with you, I presume?"

"Yes, I have a change," Heather said.

"Heather, get your dry things from your backpack and when you're ready to take off your clothes, I will turn my back. And when you're finished, then I will change. Okay?"

She climbed onto the bank and he followed. She walked behind a tree and untucked her loose fitting shirt. The bottom of the shirt hung down low and she slipped off her capris, and then her underwear. Hans wondered if she had any idea how little protection the tree provided. She bent down, carefully placing her wet clothes over a rock. Her long shirt completely covered her butt, but the cut of the hem went up the sides like a traditional men's shirt, making her long legs look even longer.

She said, "I'm getting out of my wet clothes as you suggested. Now would you please hand me my pack?"

He reached for her pack and handed it to her, unable to resist looking. She slid her arms back through the sleeves of the shirt, and then she pulled a bra out from one of her sleeves. Then she began slowly to un-button her shirt. Hans knew he should turn away, but couldn't. She took the wet shirt off, standing with nothing on. He stood staring, committing every curve to memory. Her breasts were full and round, but with enough bounce to know they were obviously natural. Her waist went in, with just enough tone to give her that natural athletic look. Her hips curved out, and she had a patch of red fuzz where her legs met. He was feeling a stirring that was no longer dormant, but was becoming more and more common in recent weeks. She pulled her clothes out of her pack and looked up at him and said, "What are you doing? You know you need to get out of those wet clothes before you catch a cold."

She took a small hand towel out of her personal pack and used it to dry off. It almost felt as if she were intentionally delaying dressing. She looked over at him, caught him watching, and smiled. Her smile was so unnerving at times. Especially times such as these.

"Hans, you really need to get out of those wet clothes."

She watched him, continuing to smile, as he began unbuttoning his shirt. He then opened his pack and pulled out a dry shirt. Then he turned away from her, quickly slipped off his pants and heard her say from behind him, "I sure can tell you do a lot of hiking, climbing and mountain biking. It's apparent by your tone."

Hans wasn't sure how to take this bold woman. He quickly dressed with his shirt untucked to hide his erection. He turned around, to see she was also dressing, buttoning up a dry shirt, and then she stepped into a pair of slacks. Even though the show was over, his reaction did not quickly subside.

They gathered their wet clothes and rolled them inside a poncho and then continued on the trail. The dampness of their hair became more noticeable as the daylight began to diminish and the coolness of the evening closed in on them before they reached the village of Erlenbach. They were now below the castle, and it was just a short climb to the castle gate. The first thing Hans did was to inquire about a room, but there was no vacancy. Heather was anxious to investigate the castle, but thought it better to wait until the following day when she was rested.

"Come," said Hans. "We'll go down to the village and inquire about accommodations there."

After checking with several pensions he learned that the May Day festivities were about to begin and all available rooms had been booked for some time. While Heather waited on a park bench, Hans kept asking and found a single room at the Gaststätte Zum *Bewartstein*. It was a small hotel with a restaurant and a view of the castle. Someone had just cancelled their reservation and he was in luck. He went to get Heather.

"Apparently the May Day festivities are the reason for the lack of rooms. I failed to consider that when planning this trip. We still have the option of camping out," he said smiling.

"A festival?" asked Heather. "Does that mean that they are all sold out?"

Hans held up the key and said, "They are now. We were lucky enough to show up just as someone cancelled their reservation."

Heather looked at the single key and said, "One room?"

"Yes, just one room," Hans replied. "I went ahead and took it. I don't believe there are any other rooms to be had."

Heather nodded, saw the restaurant, and said, "What if we go upstairs, take our wet clothes and hang them out, and then come back down here to the restaurant for something to eat."

Hans nodded and said, "That sounds like a good idea. The raising of the May Pole will start soon. If we hurry we can watch it. Would you like to see it?"

"Yes, of course. It sounds like fun."

Once they got inside the room, Hans was surprised that Heather's bold behavior from this afternoon suddenly seemed subdued. She pulled her damp clothes rolled up in the poncho out of her back pack, hung them up and said, "I'm ready to go when you are."

When Hans finished hanging up his damp clothes they went down and out to the street. They walked to the center of the village where a large crowd of people had gathered and were already eating and drinking while the local band was playing upbeat songs for the occasion. Without asking, Hans ordered two mugs of beer and two bratwursts. He handed Heather the mug of beer and said, "Prost."

Heather took the mug and said "Prost." They tapped their mugs together and then took a large swallow. Hans watched as she wiped the foam from her mouth. Even that seemed sensual.

Heather was more relaxed now that she was among the crowd. Suddenly the Band struck up a lively chord as the *Feuerwehr*, the village firemen, came marching into the center carrying the May Pole. It was not really a pole, but a long birch tree with the branches still intact at the top decorated with multiple colored ribbons.

As a drum roll began, the pole was raised using ropes and ladders to assist. When the tree reached its full upright position, the crowd applauded. The band then began playing *Ein Prosit*, and everyone raised their mugs of beer, or glasses of wine, to toast the event.

Heather found this event interesting and fun. In fact she showed no signs of wanting to return to the hotel and their room, even though they were both tired. Hans realized that she was stalling, and found her behavior perplexing and slightly amusing at the same time. For all her bold behavior at the stream, she was apprehensive.

He said, "I hope you don't mind too terribly about the room. I felt it was our only opportunity to have a decent night's sleep and to let our clothes dry out."

"No, no," she stammered, "I don't have a problem. It was the only option."

Hans decided to test his theory and said, "Well, after the stream today, I didn't think...."

Heather interrupted and said, "Look Hans, just because I am not modest, doesn't mean...."

Hans quickly added, "That you wouldn't mind if I slept on the floor in the same room."

Heather smiled and Hans could see the look of relief wash over her. In a way he was disappointed, yet he, too, was relieved.

She said, "You know, I am getting rather tired."

"Yes, me, too. We had a long walk today."

Hans took her arm and they headed back to their room. Without further conversation, Heather went into the bathroom. After her shower she came out in a nightshirt.

Hans then took his shower. When he came out, he was surprised to see that Heather had taken some of the blankets off the bed along with the sleeping bags from the backpack and had created a very inviting place for him to sleep.

He smiled and said, "Very nice, but don't you need some blankets?"

"I have sheets and that should be enough. I just want to make sure you are comfortable, being as gallant as you are."

He nodded as he knelt on the floor and slid into the make shift bed she had prepared. He pulled up the covers and turned on his side.

She climbed into the bed, turned out the light, and said in a soft whisper, "*Gute Nacht*, Hans."

Heather couldn't see his smile as he replied, "*Gute Nacht*, Heather."

Exhausted, Hans quickly fell asleep. He wasn't sure what time it was when he heard the sound of teeth chattering. He sat up from his warm but uncomfortable makeshift bed and saw her curled up in a little ball, the sheets gathered around her and her teeth chattering. He could feel the coolness in the room. It was the time of the year when heaters were already turned off and the nights could be cold. He got up, took his blanket and placed it over her. He heard her whisper, "Thank you, Hans."

Hans went back to his bed on the floor and climbed into the sleeping bag. The extra padding from the blanket was greatly missed. Sleep did not come easily as he listened to the continued sounds coming from Heather. This time she was mumbling, and whispering. From the tone, it sounded like she was talking to someone she loved.

***

Heather was exhausted, and as soon as Hans gave her the blanket, she fell fast asleep. She was surprised how easily she fell asleep with Hans sleeping on the floor beside her. Dreams came quickly, and were of the castle and the girl. Something was going on. Her father was talking to another knight, and she wasn't sure what was going on. Her Champion sent a note asking to meet her at a secret location. She met him and they talked. Her Champion had heard that her father was discussing marriage terms with another. It did help to explain the looks she was getting from her father and this other knight. They tried to think of a way to prevent the marriage. Her Champion was not in a position to offer marriage, not just yet. Then she said, "What if I give myself to you?"

Heather woke with a start to the sound of her own voice mumbling those words. She looked over at Hans, his back turned to her. Thank goodness he didn't hear her say those words.

CHAPTER ELEVEN
BEWARTSTEIN

The next morning Hans and Heather woke early. Hans waited until Heather was finished in the bathroom. When he had finished getting ready, he said, "I trust you slept well last night."

"Yes, very well. Thank you for asking."

Hans was tempted to make some comment about talking in her sleep, but then changed his mind. Instead he went to the door and said, "Shall we?"

They went downstairs for breakfast. As they were having their coffee, Heather pulled out her sketches and shared them with Hans. She said, "You know, I think I might know where to look for the note."

Intrigued, Hans asked, "Where might that be?"

"Well, so far both notes have been found in the upstairs room in what appeared to be guest quarters."

"There are a number of guest quarters at *Bewartstein*."

"Yes, I know. I went there myself once, but was not successful."

Hans watched as she overlaid her sketches carefully on the map, she was thinking not of the individual castles, but in three dimensions as they related to one another. "See, I thought they all might have been in the northwest room or the north room, since *Landeck* and *Madenburg* are in close proximity. The notes were found in the northwest and north rooms of each castle, so I focused most of my searching to those corners of *Bewartstein*, to no avail."

She traced her pencil sketches on the map and showed how the points came together, and then said, "Now if you look at it from this perspective, *Bewartstein* is on the far northern side. If I trace a line from *Bewartstein* back to where these other two points cross, I would need to look at the southern and southeastern rooms." She was bright, very bright. He looked at where all three lines crossed and he turned white... It was *Trifels*, the castle where he first found his note many years ago.

She said, "Hans, Hans are you okay? You look white as a sheet."

"Yes, I am fine." And then added, "That is rather speculative, don't you think."

She shrugged her shoulders, placed her hand under her chin and said, "It is all I have to go on."

He opened his mouth to say something, then changed his mind and said, "Well, it is better than nothing."

"That is exactly what I thought. If I am wrong, we are no worse off than we already are, and if I am right, then we are better off than we were."

Hans smiled. "What do we have to lose? Are you ready, my de…" He cleared his throat and continued, "my friend."

Heather noticed the Freudian slip and turned away to hide her smile. As they walked through town on their way to the castle, they noted that a clean up was in process from the celebrations of the night before. They walked quickly, Heather leading the way with a new level of excitement in her step.

When they arrived at the castle, she headed straight for the main tower. It was unusual that they could enter without being stopped, seeing that the castle was now in private hands. Tours were conducted regularly and it was generally not open to the public without a tour guide. Looking for the room that Heather thought might be the right room was made difficult because that section of the castle was closed for repairs.

Hans suggested that while they were there, they should go ahead and check out the other rooms. Heather reluctantly agreed. It seemed that when she had something in her mind she didn't want to be diverted. They continued their investigation of each room while Hans, trying to be a good guide, told her about the various rooms from information on the brochure. He also pointed out the huge well on the main floor that was over 100 meters deep and could likely tell some stories best left untold. There was also a torture chamber where the devices used for that purpose were still on display.

Heather appeared to be distracted the whole time. She was determined to get into the section currently closed off to the public. As the afternoon came to an end, and they had not found anything, Heather asked, "Hans, what do you think they would do if I just acted like I couldn't read the warning signs and walked back there?"

Hans was surprised by her brazen suggestion and said, "You can't just go through the barricades."

Heather gave him a determined look and with her hands on her hips said, "We walked 20 kilometers to get here, and I know the note is in that blocked off section. I want to go back and check."

Hans firmly said, "I won't be a part of this."

Heather dropped her hands from her hips and said, "I didn't ask you to. I can sneak through myself, if need be."

Hans whispered, "You can wait until tomorrow. We can come here again tomorrow."

Frustrated, Heather begrudgingly agreed to go back to the hotel and wait until the next day. Before they departed, Hans showed her a huge underground tunnel that had been carved out by hand. There was no daylight and they used candles to walk through this hidden passage. The chisel marks were a reminder of the hard labor needed to accomplish this task.

That night they went out and enjoyed the festivities of May Day. Heather seemed distracted and distant. When they sat down for dinner, Heather asked, "Why do you have to be so old fashioned?"

Hans snapped back, "Do you mean law-abiding? Or even better, respectful of other people's property, country, and culture?"

Heather stared at him, "Are you saying I am being disrespectful?"

"You are acting like a typical American tourist who thinks that rules don't apply to them."

"Typical American," Heather repeated audibly. "If I remember correctly, you are also an American."

"Yes, and I have spent the past twenty years trying to avoid appearing like an ugly or arrogant American."

She lifted her head haughtily, "So that's what I am, an ugly American. I am so glad that we could clear that one up."

Abruptly she stood and stomped away from the table. He watched her as she went to the front desk and began talking to the desk clerk. Hans suspected she was trying to get her own room. Then he saw the Clerk make a notation and hand her a room key.

She walked back over to Hans and said, "If you don't mind, I would like to get my things out of your room."

She turned without further comment and headed up the stairs. Taking his time, Hans paid the cashier and then proceeded to the room. He wasn't going to give her the satisfaction of rushing up behind her and opening the door. She could wait outside the room for all he cared.

When he got to the room, there was a note that said, "The maid let me inside. I have my things. I guess not everyone considers me an ugly American."

Hans knew that Heather was angry with him, but the truth was he was annoyed with her. She still had that American mentality, "I'm-an-American-and-can-do-what-I-please-despite-some-silly-foreign-rules" attitude that he had spent half his life trying to change. Yet although the bed was much more comfortable than the floor, Hans did not sleep well.

CHAPTER TWELVE
THE NOTE AT *BEWARTSTEIN*

Heather woke early the next morning. She was going to show Hans that she could do things her way. She arrived at the castle just as it was opening and found the curator, a small man who stood a good six inches shorter than Heather, with a round ball-shaped build, complete with a bald head and pale, pasty skin. She walked up to him and said with proper German, "*Guten Morgen. Sprechen Sie Englisch?*"

The curator said, "Yes, yes, I speak English."

Heather said, "My name is Heather Wilson, from the San Francisco firm of Kranshaw, Martin and Wilson. I am on a sabbatical studying the ancient castles of Europe and this castle has brought me all the way across the globe." Then she smiled with the sultriest smile she could muster.

The curator was pleased to provide Heather with a personal tour. She shared her sketches with him, and asked if she could do one from one of the rooms in *Bewartstein*.

"But of course, my dear lady. You will notice that some areas are under repair and it may be good to avoid those areas."

Heather knew exactly which rooms she wanted to investigate and sketch. The trick was going to be how to convince the curator to allow her to do her sketches in the closed rooms. Heather interrupted and said, "I'm sorry, sir, but that is the area that I am particularly interested in. I'm sure I wouldn't disturb anything just to look, would I?"

He said, "Those sections are currently in repair; you would not be interested in them."

Heather replied, "My dear sir, as an architect, it is not only the dream of structure and purpose, but it is in watching it become reality that brings the greatest joy. I am familiar with construction sites, and it is the architect in me that wants to look at the construction methods, and what better time than when they are under construction."

She could tell he was almost convinced, so then she said, "I will draw you a sketch like these," She held out her sketches, "for display, if you would like."

The curator hesitated, and then said reluctantly, "Okay. But you will be especially careful. I wouldn't want any harm to come to you. The workers leave all kinds of things lying around that
could cause injury."

Heather gave him her charming smile and said, "I'll be very careful. I don't want to take up too much of your time. I can do my sketch alone, if you don't mind. If I have any questions, I can come and get you. Is that agreeable?"

The curator wasn't too pleased to leave her alone, especially in the work area, but reluctantly acquiesced.

Heather started immediately with the chambers that resembled those found at *Burg Landeck*. She was methodical in her investigation, not wanting to overlook anything. She found nothing in the first chamber. When she entered the second chamber she felt a sensation. She was drawn to a corner of the room where a ledge protruded from the wall. It looked like it was used as a seat. She sat down and felt under the seat. As her hand carefully moved over each indentation, she stopped. There was something loose. She knelt down and looked at the area, and there was a piece of paper visible. She brushed away the mortar around it and carefully removed the paper. "Yes!" She exclaimed out loud. "The note!" She didn't bother to open it, but tucked it away in her purse. So as not to create any suspicion, she pulled out her sketchpad and created a sketch of the room. However, her sketch went beyond the current state of the room, to a dream of what the room could have been like in its days of grandeur. It was as though her pencil was guiding her to add tapestries displaying a crest of arms, and other details giving the sketch a lived in look. Pleased with her sketch, she packed up her pad, and slowly made her way around the construction area and then out to where the curator was waiting.

"Thank you so much for your help," she said as she approached him. Then she opened her sketchbook and presented him with her sketch.

He looked at the sketch, then back at Heather, and said, "Amazing! Are you sure you have not been in those rooms before?"

Heather said, "No, I have not. Why?"

He pulled out a picture of the castle, from before they began their restoration. On the wall of the room was a damaged and thread bare tapestry, in the exact location where Heather had drawn it. It was hard to make out the exact pattern from the faded picture, but it was clear that the tapestry hung just as Heather had sketched it, and the crest, although thread bare, was the exact same crest as Heather had sketched.

Heather said, "I must have seen a picture of that crest somewhere."

The curator smiled and said, "Yes, it was throughout the castle." He stared at the sketch and said, "This is truly a wonderful sketch, and it feels so rich and authentic."

Heather handed it to him and said, "It is yours to keep. Thank you so much for letting me see those rooms."

"It was my pleasure, madam," he replied. "Is there anything else I can help you with?"

"No, that will be all for today. The castle is lovely and has so much history. I must be on my way. Good-bye -- or, rather, *Auf Wiedersehen*."

"*Auf Wiedersehen*," replied the curator.

Heather hurried back to the hotel. She was so excited about finding the note that her anger with Hans was completely forgotten. When she reached the hotel, she was disappointed to find that Hans was not there. She inquired at the front desk and learned that he had taken a walk with no indication as to where or when he would return.

Heather went to her room and decided to open the note. It was exciting to see that it was genuine and that it might provide the answer they were looking for. She realized that she was thinking in terms of both of them, but now she was alone. Her attempt to translate the note was not going very well at all. She needed Hans. Her thoughts were now about Hans. She wondered where he could be. He would not just up and leave her. She suddenly had a feeling of loss. "What if I lost him? What have I done? How could I have been so insensitive? Oh, Hans, please forgive me, Hans," she said as tears began to run down her cheeks. "I love you, Hans," she said softly as she heard a knock on her door.

"Who's there?" inquired Heather.

"It's me. Hans. I need to talk to you."

"Just one moment," said Heather. She quickly wiped her face and looked into the mirror. She didn't want Hans to see that she had been crying. She also brushed her hair and then opened the door. Hans was wearing his backpack.

"Hello, Hans. Come in."

"No, I won't come in. I'm sorry to disturb you and just wanted to say that I need to return home. You can accompany me if you wish, or I will arrange for your transportation back when you are ready."

"You're angry with me, aren't you Hans?"

Her direct question took him off guard. Yes, he was angry, or was it that he was just very perturbed?

"Why should I be angry?" he asked.

"Hans, I want to apologize to you for being such a fool. Won't you please step inside?"

Hans hesitated and then said, "I accept your apology. Now we must go."

"It is late in the afternoon, too late to start back. Please, Hans," she begged, "Come in. I need to show you something."

Hans felt her tugging at his heart, the softness in her voice, the gentle plea. She needed him. His anger subsided, even though he was still annoyed with her. He walked in, and as she pulled the door closed behind him he wondered if he had passed the point of no return.

She was right about the late start; it was already three in the afternoon, and a start this late would surely mean finding another room, or more likely camping out. He had already checked out of his room and wondered if he could get another.

He looked at her room. It was an upgrade from the one he had and included a sofa and desk with several books opened.

Heather said, "Thank you for stopping by, and thanks for agreeing to come in." The sincerity of her words and her tone made him feel a bit more forgiving. Then she said, "You were right, Hans. I was wrong for acting so ugly, like a bull in a china shop. It was so unacceptable. I was approaching the situation in the wrong way."

Hans said, "I am glad you understand. It reflects badly on both of us." Heather touched his forearm and said, "Yes, you are so right. Have a seat, Hans."

Hans looked at the sofa and sat on the end closer to the door. She sat down on the other end. He detected something in her mannerisms. Was it a defensive posture or something else? He was suddenly uneasy.

Looking up, then down as if asking for forgiveness, she whispered, "You were right, Hans. My idea to sneak into the area under construction was completely wrong." She hesitated and said, "So I tried another approach."

"Exactly what are you talking about, Heather?" Hans asked.

Heather cleared her throat and said softly, "I convinced the curator, a nice elderly gentleman, to allow me to go into the area under construction."

Hans's anger immediately turned to jealousy and he replied sharply, "Exactly how did you do that? Did you tell some fanciful tale about your destinies being tied together, or take the bold approach and just unbutton your shirt?"

She stood up, pointed towards the door and said, "Hans, I think it is best you leave now." It was good to see she was insulted by his comment.

Hans stood up and said, "I take it you found the note, and that's what you wanted to tell me."

Heather still pointing towards the door, said, "I asked you to leave."

Hans started walking towards the door and said, "Heather, if you need help translating it, I will be back in my village, and I will do it willingly. I find this all interesting. There is no need to try and lure me into helping you with your quest." He started walking towards the door. Suddenly Heather moved quickly and stood between him and the door.

She put both of her hands on her hips and said, "What do you mean by lure?"

He replied, "The talk of destiny, and the undressing at the creek, admittedly, was an enjoyable distraction, but not at all necessary. I find the quest for the notes interesting in and of itself."

Her hands dropped from her hips and she said, "Hans, luring you to help with my quest was never my intent. I was simply caught up in the fantasy of it all, and I don't know what I was thinking. It was truly out of character for me. I will avoid such uncomfortable encounters in the future." She held her hand out and offered it and said, "Friends?"

He shook her hand, and said, "Friends."

Then Heather said, "Are you sure I cannot talk you into translating the note? I have started to translate it, but my German is still rudimentary at best."

Hans looked at his watch. It was almost four in the afternoon, and it was too late to set out on a journey at this time. He said, "Okay, let me see it."

The two of them sat down at her desk, and she showed him her first cut at the translation.

He looked at it with a critical eye and said, "You have a good start, let me see what I can do."

After working on it for some time with Heather standing over his shoulder, he said, "I think this is it."

"My father informed me that a deal is being brokered for my marriage. Excited that my father had brokered a deal with my Champion, I rushed to meet my future husband, only to find that my future husband is a wealthy noble man from across the valley, who is grotesque in every way. I cannot, I will not marry this man. I love my Champion. I have sent a note to my Champion, that I will leave my chamber door unlatched. I will give myself to him tonight. As a soiled dove, I will no longer be suitable for marriage. By the time we make the games in Altdahn, I am sure my intended will break off our engagement."

As Hans finished reading the passage, Heather felt a chill. She looked at Hans and said, "Oh, my, what a horrible turn, being forced to marry a man she doesn't love."

Hans replied, "It was a pretty common practice among nobles of the time."

Heather got a mischievous grin and said, "This girl was a rebel."

Hans said, "Why do you say that?"

"Think about it, Hans. She is going against the system to get the man she loves."

"And she is jeopardizing her family's position and fortune because she thinks she is in love. It is hormones." Hans stated.

Heather looked at Hans and said, "Boy, you are the practical one."

"Speaking of practical, I better get down to the front desk and see if they still have my room."

Heather said, "Hans, would you like to go see the chamber where I found the note? The curator was very impressed with my sketch. He might let us in if I told him you were a colleague. It wouldn't be a lie. You are a colleague in my quest for the notes."

Hans nodded, "Yes, it would be interesting to see where you found the note, but we need to be there early, and leave early; I do have business I must attend to back in Klingenmünster."

Heather smiled and said, "Okay, bright and early tomorrow morning it is."

Hans went downstairs and found that once again they were out of rooms. He had limited choices. Go back to Klingenmünster and camp along the way - a suitable and practical choice given his situation, or go back to Heather's room. The latter was out of the question. But he would need to explain to Heather in person that he was canceling their trip back to the castle.

He walked back up the stairs and knocked lightly. She answered the door in her nightshirt, and she said enthusiastically, "Hans, what a pleasant surprise."

"There are no rooms available, so I will be heading to Klingenmünster this evening. I'm sorry to cancel our side trip back to the castle."

"It is already dark, Hans. You can stay here. I even have a sofa for you to sleep on. We are just friends, remember?"

Hans said, "I don't think it is. . .."

Heather interrupted, "It is not like the first time we stayed the night in the same room. Besides, you promised to make arrangements for my return. You won't be able to do that once you are on the trail."   Using his promise, Heather convinced him to stay.

It was not a restful night. Hans continued to think of Heather sleeping in the bed next to him. They might call each other friends, but deep in his heart he knew it was more.

The next morning they awoke early, grabbed a *Brötchen* on the way out of the hotel, and made their way to the castle.

The curator immediately recognized Heather and said, "We have not stopped talking about your sketch, and in fact we have decided to use your sketch as a template for the restoration we are doing."

Heather smiled, "I would like you to meet a colleague of mine, Hans Hess. Would it be possible for me to show him the chamber? It has so much potential."

The curator said, "Of course, absolutely. If there is anything you need, just let me know. "

As they were walking down the hall, Hans said, "That must have been some sketch. You have this guy eating out your hands."

Heather gave him her disarming smile, and said, "It was one of my best sketches. Perhaps I can have him show it to you on the way out."

They walked through the construction zone into the chamber that Heather sketched. Hans said, "It is a well-lighted room, plenty of natural sun."

The curator's pager rang and he said, "I must go. Please stop in and see me before you go, Ms. Wilson."

"I will. Thank you."

After he left, Heather walked up to the window seat and said, "Here is where I found the note."

Hans approached and touched the wall at the same time Heather was touching the wall, and they were immediately transported to another time…

By the light of a candle she bathes and hears the latch open as she rises from her bath. She turns and greets him.

Seeing the radiance of her unclothed body, he drops to his knee, lowers his head, and says, "I am but one son from a proud and noble family. I cannot offer you riches, but I will offer you my heart and soul, if you will take my hand in marriage."

She takes his hand, and says, "Yes, yes, I will take you as my husband."

They look into each other's eyes and kiss deeply. Then she blows out the candle, and leads him to her bed.

They lie side by side, slowly and ever so gently exploring each other's bodies. Her Champion takes off his shirt, and then his tights. They fight the desire to rush to completion, as they take their time, tracing the outline of each other's curves, breaking for a deep kiss. Finally his hand traces around her full round breasts, as the heat of passion grows inside her. His finger gently traces the curvature, and then she feels her nipple rise to his touch. Each sensation is new, exciting, and mystifying.

She follows his lead, tracing the outline of his nipple. They kiss again, and he begins to kiss down her neck, until his lips reach the tiny projectile on her breast waiting to be titilated. She moans as his tongue kneads her nipple. As he gently sucks, his hand moves slowly down, between her legs. Her hand moves down below his waist and she finds him hard and throbbing. She is a bit frightened, but his fingers bring even greater feelings of pleasure.

He whispers, "I want you."

She replies, "I am yours to have, now and forever."

He lowers himself over her, and then she feels the pain followed by pleasure as they became one...

Heather and Hans heard the footsteps of the curator walking into the room, and they released their hands from the wall.

Heather looked at the curator, her face flush, and said, "We were just admiring the texture of this stone."

The curator smiled and said, "There is a legend of this room, that those truly in love need only touch the wall, and will feel the intensity of a couple making love for the first time."

Heather looked over at Hans; there was little doubt in her mind that he just felt the exact same sensations as she was feeling. She could tell by the flush in his cheeks, the sweat on his brow, and, most importantly, the bulge in his pants. He said, "I think it is time we started our hike back to Klingenmünster."

As they were leaving, the curator led them into the *Rittersaal*, the knights' eating hall, and showed Hans the sketch that Heather had made of the chamber the day before. Everything about her sketch was exactly what he remembered in his vision, from the patterns on the tapestries to the arrangements of the pillows.

"Too bad you can't come back when the castle is open. This *Rittersaal* is used as a restaurant and you would enjoy a fine meal."

Checking out of the hotel and packing their things didn't take long and they were on their way. Hans decided to take a slightly different route back, thinking that some diversion would be needed. He tried to avoid making eye contact with Heather so she would not notice his feelings. He knew he had to shake the feeling of being the Champion in the time warp, yet it was too real to disregard. The feelings were real, as well as the images that kept popping up in his mind.

As they made their way along the trail, Hans would point out certain things just to make conversation. From time to time, he would observe Heather as she followed him, remaining silent except in short responses to his comments. She had such a peaceful look about her, as though she were completely contented. Why had this wonderful woman suddenly come into his life? He had his life under control and accepted his fate. Now it was all turned upside down. His sexual feelings that had long been passive were now coming alive. Were they real or imagined? Was he being a fool to think that Heather could have feelings for him in the way that he had for her? The age difference. Ah, yes. Certainly the age gap would be important to her. She was so young and vital and would require much sexual prowess to be satisfied. How could he hope to satisfy her?

What am I thinking? I'm a married man! He thought to himself. *How can I possibly entertain these thoughts?*

As Hans walked along, he felt he must find a way to extricate himself from the position he now found himself in. *She knows I'm married, she must,* he thought. *But what if she doesn't? I did tell her that no one was waiting for me at home. Would she still be interested if she knew I was married? Would she*

116

be satisfied with having a relationship that could not be permanent? No, it has gone far enough. I will help her as promised but keep my distance.

The trail took a sharp turn and just beyond was *Marthas Quelle*. Hans stopped and placed his backpack down and cupped his hands to take a drink from the spring.

"You're drinking that water? Aren't you afraid of germs?"

"No, this is pure and cool spring water. Come, try it."

Heather hesitated briefly and then went to the spring and cupped her hands and quenched her thirst. "Hans. It tastes so good. What a wonderful place this is. Can we rest a bit before continuing?"

"Of course."

Hans placed his backpack against a tree and invited Heather to do the same. She placed her backpack right next to his as they both sat down leaning against them. Heather leaned against Hans and her touch gave him a warm sensation. He didn't move away, but enjoyed the feeling of her being so close. He was deep in his own thoughts when he looked down and noticed that she had fallen asleep. He couldn't help but notice her full lips slightly parted as if waiting to be kissed. The rise and fall of her breasts reminded him of the time warp event. Visualizing his taking her for the first time and their bodies meshed as one moving in rhythm and reaching… "Stop this!" he said out loud.

Heather awoke and looked at Hans inquiringly. "Did you say something?" she asked.

"No. But now that you're awake I think we'd better be on our way. Did you rest well?"

"Oh, yes, Hans. It was so good. And I had a wonderful dream that was interrupted when I thought I heard a noise."

As they made their way along the trail, Heather asked, "Hans, what business do you have in Klingenmünster?"

Hans hesitated and then decided it was time to make sure she knew he was married, and put an end to this confusing, but exhilarating adventure. He said, "I am going to talk to a specialist about my wife's condition."

"Your wife?" Heather exclaimed. "Hans, are you married?"

Hans replied in a matter-of-voice, "Yes, of course I am married. I am wearing a wedding band, am I not?" He held up his hand.

"But you told me there was no one waiting for you at home." Heather said, with a level of desperation in her voice. "I assumed you were a widower, and that the band was in her memory."

Hans replied, "My wife is not at home. She is at a clinic. She is in a coma."

"What caused that to happen?" she asked.

"We had tried unsuccessfully to have a child, and then when Monica finally did become pregnant, the child died at birth. Monica never fully recovered from her loss. The trauma was so severe that she suffered a stroke that was diagnosed as "acute neurological injury." She slipped into a coma and didn't come out of it. She was sent to the *Pfalzklinik* since they specialize in neurological disorders.

Heather stared at him and said, "A coma, for long?"

Hans replied, "Over five years now.

"That is so sad, Hans. I'm sorry to hear that. But that still doesn't alter the fact that I have been coming on to a married man. Hans, I am so embarrassed. Oh, it explains so much, why you have been distant, reserved. Oh, I can't believe, I, I, oh, I kissed a married man. Wait a second, you kissed me, too."

Hans replied, "And the next day I wrote you a note saying that it had gone too far, remember."

JOURNEY INTO THE PAST

Heather replied, "It would have made a whole lot more sense if you would have just come right out and said, 'Hey, I can't do this. I am married'."

"I assumed you knew I was married," Hans replied innocently.

"How would I have known you were married?"

"The ring, and the fact that my nephew gave me your life story. I assumed he told you mine."

She shook her head. "What type of person do you think I am? I am not in the habit of coming on to a married man. I've been on the other side of a cheating husband. How could you think I could knowingly come on to a married man like that?"

Hans was dumbfounded. After a few moments he said, "I guess I thought you fell into the category of so many of my friends who have encouraged me to. . ."

"Cheat on your wife?" Heather replied.

Hans offered, "Get on with my life. They know the prognosis isn't good, and she wasn't herself for many years prior to the coma."

Heather looked at him, "What do you mean, wasn't herself?"

"Unresponsive, listless, fragile," he replied.

Heather asked bluntly, "Too fragile for intimacy?"

Hans turned, obviously uncomfortable with the conversation.

Heather said, "How many years has it been, Hans?"

Hans said, "I am not comfortable talking about this." He walked quickly down the trail.

Heather caught up to him, planted herself in front of him along the path, blocking his way, and said, "Hans, how many years?"

Hans replied, "She's been in a coma for five years."

Heather stared at him. "Five years and there hasn't been anyone else?"

Hans responded, "I have been successful in controlling those urges." He wanted to say until now, but thought better of it.

"Five years. You should be getting some type of reward. I was out of town for two weeks, when my husband . . ." She stopped.

Hans said, "I am not a young man. It is easier to control. My sex drive isn't what it once was."

She smiled with a half grin, "Boy you must have been something when your sex drive was at its peak. That kiss of yours knocked me for a loop."

"Let me rephrase. My sex drive wasn't what it once was until recently, very recently." Hans smiled. "I can't believe I just said that."

Heather replied, "I am glad you did. I was beginning to feel really bad thinking I was coming on to this guy who had no interest and I was totally misreading his signals. I have been out of the dating scene for quite a while."

Heather headed down the trail. After a while she said, "Five years. You know, your friends were right. You really do need to get on with your life, or at least find some companionship."

Hans said, "I am not a young man any longer."

She replied, "You seem to be doing just fine on these trails. I have little doubt you could..." She stopped.

Hans said, "Oh, no, you don't. You made me spill my guts. What were you going to say?"

She felt the color and heat fill her cheeks as she said, "That you could satisfy a woman."

He looked at her with a slight grin and said, "And why do you think that?"

"Men, I swear. They think women want all this acrobatic and athletic prowess, when it is really about the kiss, the touch, and the tenderness leading up to the act that makes it memorable. And, Hans Hess, you have the kiss."

Hans just looked at her. It took a great deal of restraint to resist taking her into his arms and kissing her. They stared into each other's eyes for a moment, and then she turned and quickly headed down the trail.

When they reached Klingenmünster, Hans asked Heather if she would go the rest of the way by herself. "I must stop by the *Klinik* and see my wife. There are things I wish to discuss with her."

"How will you discuss things with your wife if she is in a coma?"

"I didn't say she would understand or comprehend what I'm saying, but I do talk with her about what I'm doing, et cetera. I have no idea if she can hear or understand, but I have been doing that for so long that it seems normal. At least she doesn't talk back to me," he said with a smile.

"Yes," Heather said with a chuckle. "There must be some advantages to silence, I suppose."

Heather waved goodbye and Hans went to the *Klinik*. Gretchen was at her post as usual. And before Hans could ask her the question, she said "*Noch nicht*, Herr Hess."

"*Danke*, Gretchen."

Hans entered the room and the nurse departed so that he would have his privacy. He looked at his wife who lay peacefully still. He sat down on the bed and placed his hand over hers and tried to remember what it had been like when she was well and alert. There was no response to his touch and the hand felt limp and lifeless. As he looked at her, he thought about their times together before the illness. They had been happy. There had been an attraction, naturally, otherwise they would never have gotten married, but when had things changed? Was it he who had changed or was it she? The excitement of their marriage seemed to wane, and over time it became the norm just to be content with each other without any passion. Of course, that's normal, isn't it, he thought? And when did he lose interest in her in a passionate way? Of course he loved her as a person. But could he say he was "in love" with her? Perhaps that was why the passion disappeared. But whose fault was that? Was it he who was responsible? Did she not respond because he was no longer loving or compassionate with her? Or was it that she no longer showed affection toward him? He remembered how she used to come up to him for no reason whatsoever and hug him and kiss him. And he always responded. Then she stopped doing that. Why? Did she no longer love him? Had she found someone else? Something must have caused her to lose interest in him. Could it have been a physical deficiency? Was it because she became frigid that she lost interest in him? It would be so good to ask her why. What happened? But now she couldn't answer that question and probably never would.

"My dear," he said. "I must confess to you that I have fallen in love with another woman. It is not something that I planned to do. It just happened. Can you understand that?" He paused and observed her lifeless body. Certainly she would understand, wouldn't she?

"I haven't told this person that I love her, just yet. I needed to discuss it with you first. I do not plan to leave you. How could I? You have done nothing wrong to deserve my leaving you. But surely you can understand how lonely I've been over the past years. Can't you my dear?" Again he paused as though waiting for a response. For a moment, he thought he saw a slight movement around her eyes, but then dismissed that as an involuntary muscle movement.

"I have missed making love to you. I know that you didn't seem that keen on lovemaking before you became ill, but there was some tenderness associated with it and it fulfilled a physical need in me. Can you realize that I have physical needs? Would you knowingly deprive me of that fulfillment?" Again, he thought there was a twitch around the eyes. He concentrated very hard, but then thought it must have been an illusion.

"Her name is Heather. That is a nice name, isn't it? She is very caring and I think she loves me. But I have no idea how she will react when I tell her that I cannot leave you. She may think it is wrong or somehow indecent to have a physical relationship without any permanency attached to it. Would you mind very much if I made love to her? It would not be simply to satisfy a physical need, but because I do love her. She has caused me to feel so young again. I feel so attached to her. Can you understand that?"

There was no reaction of any kind, and Hans realized that he was simply talking out loud. Whether it was to relieve his own conscience that he felt the need to confess, he couldn't be sure, but it made him feel much better. Now if only Heather would understand. Would she want him the way he was without any commitment, or would she pack up and leave once the quest for the clues came to an end?

CHAPTER THIRTEEN
LISTENING AT THE WINDOW

Heather started to return to the pension. Hans Hess had left her in a quandary. She was obviously attracted to him in a way that was hard to explain. But he was married. How could she have not known? Did she miss the obvious clues? She only had seen him by himself, but he wore a ring. He had told her no one was waiting at home and hadn't lied to her. He had taken time to spend with her, but what choice did he have? Spending countless hours in a facility? He had never made the first move, and he did try to distant himself after their first kiss. She decided that she needed some answers and she wasn't going to find them at the pension. She watched the direction in which Hans was going, went around the block, and then followed him. She watched as he entered the Klinik and then she quietly slipped around the building until she heard his voice coming from one of the open windows. She crouched next to the window behind a bush, and listened to Hans' confession, where he basically asked permission to make love to her.

She waited until after Hans left the room, then peered into the window and saw the woman resting peacefully in her bed. Monica was a classic beauty with dark hair and features, but she looked so frail. She didn't move or twitch, although she was clearly breathing on her own. Heather's heart went out to Hans seeing the woman he loved in this condition day after day and now struggling with his new feelings for her. She couldn't stop thinking about that kiss, those visions; she couldn't stop thinking of Hans. How could I have these thoughts about a married man? She wondered. Yet people around town seemed to be happy that he was with another woman. She remembered the smiles she received from the restaurant owner when they called each other by their first names. They knew what he had gone through, knew his plight, and seemed genuinely happy for him. He had been devoted to his wife all these years, and I had tempted him. What type of person am I? How could I have romantic feelings towards a married man, after what happened to me? Yes, it was different. I wasn't in a coma for five years, or too fragile for intimacy. Far from it, I had been passionate most of my marriage; yes, there were times when my job took me away mentally and even physically. But it was my job that allowed us to live the lifestyle we had.

She thought of Tom's parents. Sure, they had money, and Tom was used to living in a certain lifestyle. However, other than the occasional present, they had never seen a dime of Tom's family's fortune. Her career had paid for a lifestyle she never wanted.

Tom had spent most of their marriage trying to find himself. He would either stay at home, go to college part time, get a job for a while only to hate it and quit, and even when he did have a job, it never paid enough to cover his expensive hobbies. No, he was perfectly willing to live off of her, and as the years went by, she lost respect for him, and began to resent the fact that she paid his way. Maybe Tom sensed her resentment. Maybe it was Tom's nature to stray, but stray he did. She forgave early indiscretions, blaming herself, and trying harder to be the type of woman Tom wanted. She had tried to keep the marriage together, but that became one sided. She still had hopes that Tom would change his mind and want a child as much as she did, but he was dead set against it.

With more time on his hands, Tom was less cautions and she caught him. He made it easy. She could have spent years resenting the fact that she supported him;instead, she found him with another, and it was easy to ask him for a divorce. It was then that she was thankful that there were no children involved. He initially tried to patch things up, but she had locked the door to reconciliation.

Admittedly, Heather reflected, I wasn't a perfect angel. If one were to ask Tom, Heather had her "relationships" too. Two in twenty years: one with a mentor and one with a co-worker. They were emotional relationships built out of admiration and mutual respect; relationships that went beyond working relationships, but never even came close to crossing that well defined line of physical intimacy. Yet, in many ways they were far more damaging to their marriage, because it was in admiring and respecting these men, and the admiration and respect given in return, that she realized what was missing in her marriage. Tom demanded that she sever her ties to these men. It was difficult, but she did it to save their marriage.

She thought of the "what-ifs," but if she had left long ago, she would not be here, now, facing her current dilemma—Hans Hess. What was she going to do about Hans Hess? He was in her thoughts and in her mind. She admired and respected Hans, and most of all she wanted to be with him. But could she get over the fact that he was married?

Suddenly the thought came to her, would he leave his wife for her? No, she wouldn't allow it. She wasn't a twenty year old any longer who needed the reassurance of a ring and a wedding. No, if anything, such institutions felt shallow to her now. If the time came, she would never ask more than he could give.

Heather slept thinking about Hans. The vision at the castle felt so real. How could either one of them deny it?

CHAPTER FOURTEEN
THE COMPROMISE

Hans was at the pension early. Heather's bedside phone rang and she learned that Hans was waiting for her in the lobby. She jumped out of bed, took a quick shower and then hurried downstairs. Her mind was spinning as to why Hans was calling on her. This is the first time he came by so early, so something must have happened. Perhaps it was something to do with his wife, and that thought brought her back to reality. Yes, he was a married man.

Hans was standing by the desk reading a newspaper when she approached. He turned, and when he saw her, she stopped. They stood looking at each other without saying a word. He looked into her eyes as if searching for something. She tried to read his thoughts and was apprehensive. Although it was just a momentary silence, it seemed longer when Hans finally said, "Good Morning, Heather."

Heather hesitated, and then said, "*Guten Morgen*, Hans."

That brought a smile to both their faces and Hans said, "Perhaps our roles have been reversed. You will speak German and I will speak English?"

"Hardly. Seems I'm getting used to certain things and haven't heard a greeting in English since I've been here. Was there some reason you greeted me in English?"

"We've got to talk, Heather. May I take you to breakfast somewhere else where we can have some privacy?"

"Of course. Let me get my sweater and I'll be right back."

Hans paced while waiting, wondering what exactly he would say to her. But talk they must if they were to continue working together.

He drove to Landau where they found a nice quiet and cozy corner in a *Kaffeehaus*. After ordering breakfast, he reached across the table and took Heather's hand in his. It was a strange feeling, and he resisted the urge to kiss her hand. He needed to keep his head and not let his emotions rule.

"Heather, I think you know that I have become fond of you since meeting you. We have spent considerable time together as a result of your quest to find the clues. . ."

"Our quest, Hans," Heather interrupted.

"Yes. It seems that it has become our quest." Hans hesitated before continuing trying to choose his words carefully. "I want to apologize to you if I misled you about being a married man." Heather was about to interrupt, but Hans raised his hand and continued. "It was presumptuous of me to think you would know I was married simply because I wore a ring. I must confess that I may have thought that by telling you, that it would affect a budding relationship, and I was enjoying our time together. I now realize what a mistake that was. You are a very special person. You are young, vital, have a profession, and once you leave here, you will continue with your life. What I'm trying to say is that I respect you and will not do anything to disrupt your life. I will continue to serve as your guide, if you wish, but only if that is your wish. And please know that I shall do my best to keep our association strictly professional."

Heather was waiting impatiently for Hans to finish, but could wait no longer. "Are you quite finished, Herr Hess?"

"It's Hans."

"If you wish to become so formal with me, perhaps I should call you 'Mr.' or *Herr*, instead. You know nothing about my feelings or me. You are making lots of assumptions, and I think that is most unfair. Yes, I have a profession and have been successful at what I do. And I have been married before, as I told you. That freedom allowed me to jump on a plane and come here. I am not totally free, since I have professional responsibilities, but it does allow me time to do the things I want to do and the means to do them."

"I admire you for that, Heather. You are an unusual person. Intelligent, energetic with a zest for life, and beauty, as well." Heather blushed as Hans continued. "Someone who has much to offer the right person - a person worthy of your talents. And…"

"Hans, you're doing it again. You are making assumptions about what I want out of life. You think you know me, but…"

As breakfast was served their conversation came to a halt. They began eating in silence, avoiding eye contact, both deep in thought. Finally Hans said, "Heather, I'm sorry if I have presumed things, and you're also right that I don't know you all that well. I think that goes for the both of us. Therefore, may I suggest that we take one day at a time, so to speak, and not let our emotions rule? I was going to withdraw my services as your guide, but since I've been so presumptuous about things, I shall continue, if you wish."

"I do wish, Hans." Heather replied. Then she pulled out the note and said, "So what do you think of the latest note we found?"

Somewhat relieved that the subject was changed, Hans said, "Impulsive."

Heather replied, "I would say it was romantic."

Hans said, "Romantically impulsive."

Heather smiled and repeated, "Romantically impulsive, I like that." And then she said, "And I think our young couple acted in a romantically impulsive nature."

"I suspect you might be right," as he thought of the vision of the couple making love.

"So, I wonder if they will live happily ever after."

Hans looked down and said, "It is probably unlikely."

"Come on, Hans, have some hope. So what is our next castle?"

"*Altdahn.* It is about 22 kilometers from here."

"How soon do you think we can go to *Altdahn*?"

Hans thought for a moment. "I would like to take a couple of days and actually plan the trip, including making reservations for lodging. I would prefer not to be in the situation we found ourselves in at Erlenbach."

Heather smiled while stifling a chuckle and said, "So you don't want to sleep on the floor again?"

"No, and I prefer not to sleep on a sofa, either."

Heather chuckled and said, "You are such a gentleman, Hans."

Hans blushed, but smiling said, "Thank you." He looked at his watch and said, "I must be going. Shall we meet tomorrow and discuss plans to travel to *Altdahn*?"

Heather was a bit disappointed that she would have to wait until the next day to see Hans again, but she said, "Yes, that sounds wonderful. In the meantime I will study my travel books and hopefully come up with some ideas, as well."

Hans paid for the meal and drove back to her pension, dropping her off at the curb.

Heather went up to her room and began going through the travel books trying to find someplace to offer as a suggestion; Hans had been making all the arrangements. While she enjoyed his guided trips, she thought just once she would like to make a suggestion. She turned her book to the Dahn area, and immediately saw a review on the *Hotel und Vitalresort Pfalzblick*, a four-star health resort. The place sounded absolutely wonderful. It was just a couple of kilometers from Altdahn with scenic views from every room. It was probably not exactly what Hans would have in mind, but the idea of going to a health resort for three or four days sounded wonderful.

She had been relatively frugal on her vacation so far. Hiking or riding bikes to the different castles, staying at a pension which was much more reasonable than hotels, and then Hans' seeming determination to pay for their meals out. She had budgeted for her and Tom to spend a couple months in the South Pacific at four-star resorts, chartering sailboats to travel between islands. Her trip to Germany for just herself was significantly less expensive than the trip she had planned and budgeted.

It was time she splurged a little. It was time she treated her guide, Hans. She called the resort hotel and without hesitation booked two rooms for three nights each with a spa package. Perhaps if he relaxed in a hot tub or sauna, he might shed some of his inhibitions, if only temporarily. Perhaps if they both relaxed in a hot tub. Heather's mind wondered about the possibilities, and she smiled. She hoped Hans would not be too upset.

The next morning, Hans called her room early. Heather was bursting with excitement. She couldn't wait to tell him of her plan and wondered how he would take it.

Hans was standing by the desk reading a newspaper when she approached. He turned, and when he saw her, she stopped. They stood looking at each other without saying a word. Although it was just a momentary silence, it seemed longer when Hans finally said, "Good Morning, Heather."

Heather hesitated, and then said, "*Guten Morgen*, Hans."

It was a repeat of the day before, yet each time she saw him she felt butterflies in her stomach.

She smiled and said, "Shall we go somewhere for breakfast? I have an idea I would like to share with you."

They drove to Bad Bergzabern, a health resort town not too far from Klingenmünster with lots of eating places and sidewalk cafes. Hans selected a café in the *Fussgängerzone,* the pedestrian-only zone, off limits to vehicular traffic, that had a nice outside terrace and afforded the opportunity to watch people going about their morning shopping. After they were seated and ordered, Hans said, "You mentioned that you had an idea you would like to share."

"I read through my books on Dahn and found this wonderful place."

Hans interrupted, "There are a number of pensions and even a couple of hotels."

"I'm sure there are, but did you know that there is also a spa resort hotel there? I would like to try it Hans. It is called *Vitalresort Pfalzblick.*"

"My, you have been busy. Yes, I've heard of it, but have never been there. If that is what you'd like to do, why not? I'll call and make reservations."

"I've already done that and have booked two rooms. It's all set," Heather said with a big smile. "You don't mind that I have done this, do you Hans?"

"No. Of course not. It is a surprise that you have taken such initiative." Heather was about to interrupt; however, realizing that his remark may have been a bit insulting, he added, "I realize you are a take charge person based on your profession. It's just a bit unusual for me to have someone do things for me. You are always full of surprises."

CHAPTER FIFTEEN
THE SPA

Instead of hiking to Dahn, Hans decided to drive. He wanted to show her more of the country, especially the small villages. After breakfast, he took Heather back to her pension to pack some clothes and he went home to do the same. He selected casual wear and one suit for eveningwear, just in case.

Heather was excited when Hans picked her up. Her smile was contagious, and before long they were both laughing about silly things. Hans would interrupt their conversation to point out things of interest as they drove along.

"You'll notice that between each village there is either forest or farmland. There are no houses dotting the landscape."

"That's odd, isn't it?" asked Heather.

"It's a conservation thing. Preserving land for farming as well as needed forests. You've probably noticed that homes are clustered within small villages where services are available. That includes bus transportation and in larger areas, trains service as well. There are still people who don't own a car here. Considering that the cost of gasoline is about four times what it costs in America, one can understand why public transportation is needed. You also find more fuel-efficient and smaller cars for that reason."

As they approached Dahn, Hans began to talk about the two castles in the Dahn area called *Neudahn* (New Dahn) and *Altdahn* (Old Dahn). "I hope you won't be too disappointed, since the castles are just Ruine. Did you have a chance to review the history of *Altdahn*?"

"Yes, and it is interesting. I keep reading how most castles in this region have been destroyed more than once and yet continued to rebuild and hold influence."

"*Altdahn* is actually three castles stretching 200 meters along the crest of five sandstone cliffs. They are called, *Altdahn, Grafendahn,* and *Tannstein.* They were built in the 13th century and owned by the Knights of *Altdahn,* called *Grafendahn.* That dynasty died out in 1603. Then the Bishop of Speyer laid claim to the castles as a fief, and they thus reverted back to the church. The castles were destroyed in 1689. I don't want you to be disappointed. If nothing else, we may have a few days of leisure at the spa."

They arrived at the Vitalresort hotel with a feeling of anticipation. It seemed perfect for a quiet and peaceful way to spend a few days. It had a solarium and physical fitness room that promised to be interesting, thought Hans.

The receptionist seemed puzzled that a man and women arriving together would have reserved separate rooms. They seemed to belong together, and that made it more puzzling considering that the rooms were adjoining.

They were given the keys, and Hans said that they could handle their own luggage. When they got to the rooms, Hans noted that they were side by side.

"Do you have a preference of room?" he asked.

"No, why don't you choose?" said Heather.

Hans picked one at random and when he entered, he noticed that there was a door leading to Heather's room, although it was closed. *Did she request adjoining rooms?* He wondered.

He placed his bag on the rack and then noticed that the head of his bed was directly on the wall to Heather's room. He couldn't help but wonder where her bed was located, but then he shrugged it off. *Why should it matter where her bed was located? After all, it is not in the same room.*

Having placed his clothes on hangers and tucked the rest away in the drawers, he was tempted to knock on the door to the adjoining room to see if Heather was finished, but then decided it was better to go into the hallway and knock.

Heather opened the door as soon as he knocked and invited him in. He stepped inside and the first thing he noticed was that the head of her bed was on the same wall as his, and, from what he could tell, exactly at the same location. His heart raced, but he quickly pushed the feeling aside.

"Would you like to go down and have some coffee? At this time of day, they usually have *Kaffee und Kuchen*. That is coffee with an assortment of very appetizing cakes and tortes."

"Oh, I'd love some. Yes. Shall we go?"
They entered the restaurant and went to the designated area reserved for afternoon deserts. "Ummm. Everything looks so scrumptious," said Heather. "It will be difficult to choose."

"Why don't you select what you want and then we'll be seated. It's much better to order after seeing the item than simply ordering from a menu card."

They were seated in a small alcove and the waitress appeared with the menu.

"*Zwei Kännchen Kaffee, bitte,*" Hans ordered. Then he turned to Heather and asked if she had selected what desert she would like.

"I think I would like the *Schwarzwälder Kirschtorte,*" she said.

"I'll have the same," said Hans.

To the waitress, Hans said, "*Wir hätten gerne zwei Schwarzwälder Kirschtorten.*"

"You said that you would like two orders of Black Forest Cherry Cake, right?"

"You're doing very well. The next time I want you to place your own order. The practice will be helpful."

When their desert arrived, Heather took a bite of the Black Forest Cake and her eyes closed, as if allowing all of her senses to focus on the taste.

"This is heavenly, so rich, and delightful. One simply doesn't find chocolate this rich and flavorful in the states."

Hans enjoyed watching her consume her cake; she had passion in everything she did, be it eating a slice of cake, sketching a room, or finding the clues in the castle. He considered that if she was so passionate about so many everyday things, just how passionate would she be about…he brushed the thought aside. He watched as she pushed away the half eaten cake. It surprised him, and he said, "You don't plan to finish your cake?"

"If I did finish it, I would spend the next four days in the sauna trying to burn off the calories I consumed." She paused, and then said, "I am no longer a child who feels the need to totally consume something. I realize experiencing just a taste of the richness of the moment is more fulfilling than not experiencing it all." She took another bite of the cake, closed her eyes, licked the whip cream frosting off her upper lip, and then said, "And yet sometimes it is hard to give up something once you've had a taste." The waitress came by and Heather handed the lady her plate and said, "It is wonderful, but I had to stop."

Hans swallowed hard. He wondered if Heather's statement referred to more than just cake. He was sure it did, but what exactly was she saying? Hans stared at her. He felt she was trying to tell him something, but what if he misunderstood? No, he couldn't take the risk that she was talking about anything other than cake. Finally he said, "So, what would you like to do the rest of the day? It is a bit late to visit the castles, but if you would like…"

Heather interrupted saying, "I think I would like to take a walk around the grounds; they have a wonderful private garden. I need to work off that extra bite of cake I ate," she said, winking.

"A walk in the garden sounds wonderful. I'll ask the waitress for our bill."

"I selected the all inclusive package and the meals are included. By the way, the package also includes a massage, a facial, and a bath treatment. I was thinking of doing one each morning and spread out the pampering."

"While you are being pampered, I'll do some reading. Did you see that wonderful reading room when we walked in?"

Heather smiled. Hans had noticed that she had several very distinct types of smiles: her childlike wonder smile, her everyday smile, her passionate smile, and her devious smile. This smile was definitely her devious smile as she said, "Oh, no, Hans Hess, you will be getting a facial, massage, and bath treatment, too."

Hans looked at her and said, "I don't think…"

"It is part of the package, and it is about time you had someone pamper you. You have been such a great guide; this is my gift to you." Then she summoned her child-like smile and said, "And you can't say no to a gift."

"I am still not sure. I can see a good therapeutic massage, but a facial and bath treatment?"

"Oh, no, you don't. Everyone can use a facial once in their life."

He realized he wasn't going to win this discussion so he put his napkin on the table and said, "Are you ready for that walk?"

She placed her napkin next to his, smiled and said, "Absolutely."

They got directions from the concierge and proceeded along the path to the garden. As they walked and admired the flowers in bloom, they discovered that they both liked the same types of flowers and similar fragrances. Walking side by side, their shoulders would touch, and their hands briefly brush as they weaved along the garden path. They saw other couples walking hand and hand, and, for a moment, Hans reached for Heather's hand, but then pulled back. *One day at a time. Think with your head, not your heart,* he thought to himself.

They sat in the garden terrace and watched the sun set. Heather said, "Well, I am seriously considering going for a quick swim before I shower and dress for dinner."

As they made their way inside they passed the indoor swimming pool and both of them noticed that many of the patrons using the pool were nude. Heather said, "Maybe I will pass on the swim."

Hans chuckled and said, "That puritan American upbringing. It does take some getting used to the openness here in Europe."

"I can see that," she said. And then in a teasing voice, "I don't see you rushing to the pool."

"I was raised in America, too, and some aspects of my upbringing are easier to change than others."

When they got to their rooms, Heather said, "See you at seven."

She quickly showered and allowed her hair to dry naturally. While her hair was drying she pulled out her laptop. She had promised herself not to use it on this vacation, but she just wanted to see if there were any new or different bits and pieces of information on the castles to impress Hans.

As soon as she logged on, she saw a series of emails from Karen flash up on the screen. They won a proposal that had been submitted months ago. Heather had been named managing partner because of the proposal. It was one of the long shots that every firm takes on occasionally. Intelligence in the industry said that it would go to a competitor. Heather was surprised, but happy they won. It would be a great project. At the same time it would mean an earlier than expected return to the states.

Respecting Heather's vacation and need for a respite, the senior partners had taken on the new project; the only problem was that there was a major meeting with the client in four weeks, and the clients expected Heather to be at that meeting. However, there were several emails discussing how best to approach Heather about the meeting. Heather fired off a quick email that said, "I will be there for the meeting so stop worrying. I want the presentation in my email, a week before the event. I am enjoying Germany tremendously and plan to continue to enjoy it until the day I leave for the presentation. So my cell phone is still off."

Heather sent the email, shut down and put away her computer. Suddenly she had a timeline to find the clues, and more importantly, a need to break through Hans' tough barriers.

She pulled her hair up into a soft bun allowing ringlets of curls to cascade; she put on a light coat of make-up and added some highlight around her eyes. Then she put on her royal blue evening dress, a mid-calf length, silk dress that caressed her figure with a slightly plunging halter neckline, exposing her back and shoulders. She put on a single diamond bracelet, and a teardrop single diamond necklace that fell perfectly in the center of the plunging neckline. She applied a light coat of natural lipstick, giving her lips a natural glow. She looked at her clock. It was exactly seven when she heard a knock on her door.

She rose and answered the door. Hans was waiting in a well-tailored suit that made him look even more distinguished. She smiled and said, *"Guten Abend*, Hans."

He stared at her for a moment, with almost the same look as when he accidentally saw her nude near the creek. Finally he said, *"Guten Abend*, Heather, shall we?"

He offered his arm and they strolled down the hallway to the restaurant. *She does look stunning,* he thought. It felt good to be walking with her arm holding onto his. *How long had it been since I did anything like this?* He mused. And her scent was so fresh and pleasing. *How wonderful it would be if I could just stop and embrace her. Shake it off, Hans,* he told himself.

Their table was reserved. It was customary for guests with full pension (all meals included) to have a special area for eating, and they had been given the best table with the most privacy. He wasn't sure if that had been requested or if the receptionist just made a romantic assumption. In any event, it promised to be a pleasant dinner.

As soon as they were seated, Heather leaned forward and touched Hans lightly on his arm. "Hans., I am so pleased that you agreed to come here with me. I have such a wonderful feeling about everything. This hotel, our quest, our relationship. . ." She paused and then continued, "What I mean to say is that getting to know you has been very special, and the friendship that we have is very special to me."

Heather's eyes became misty. Hans didn't know where this was leading, but was being caught up in what she was saying. He too felt the same things. It was the subject of their relationship that he was still having a problem dealing with. How far to let it go? Where would it lead? All the questions that kept holding him back from letting his true feelings show.

"Being with you is also special to me." He placed his hand over hers and they just looked into each other's eyes. He felt drawn to her. *How much longer can I resist this woman?* He wondered. He then took his hand away and diverted his eyes to the waiter.

He ordered wine. As full pension guests there was a pre-set menu with two choices. They had both ordered the same meal, and when the wine was poured, they had toasted each other a number of times for various reasons, some even very silly, causing them to laugh and sometimes blush. They were enjoying themselves immensely and hadn't looked at the clock. It was when they realized that they were the only guests remaining in the restaurant that Hans said, "I think we should go. I'd like to take a short walk around the grounds in the moonlight before bedtime. Would you like that?"

Heather was beaming and said, "Oh, yes, Hans, that would be lovely."

They walked hand in hand through the gardens. There were a few benches here and there, but most were occupied. Heather squeezed his arm as they continued walking and then she spied a vacant bench, and said, "Could we sit for a bit? Do you mind?"

"Not at all," he replied.

Before sitting down, Heather looked to the sky and said, "Hans, it is so beautiful. The moon, the stars, the wonder of it all. Do you ever wonder about space, Hans?"

"Yes, I often have. I'm no expert in matters of space, but I do know that it is boundless and that someday man will live there. Would you want to live in space, Heather?"

"Perhaps. But only with the right person. I remember as a little girl, lying on my back, looking at the sky at night and repeating the poem, 'Twinkle, twinkle little star...' it gave me such a feeling of longing." Heather put her arm around Hans's waist and he did the same, laying his arm around hers. As they both stood looking at the sky, he suddenly pulled her to him, holding her close. She responded by leaning her head on his shoulder. The feeling was electrifying. His heart was pounding and he knew she could feel it. He was about to kiss her – the urge was so strong, and then he quickly released her and said with a quiver in his voice, "Here we are standing in front of the bench instead of sitting on it. Come, Heather, sit down."

Heather did as he asked, but it was obvious that she would have preferred standing with her arms around him. After Heather sat down, Hans sat a respectful distance apart from her. They sat on the bench, hands to themselves, staring out into the night. Finally, Heather said, "Hans Hess, you have to be the most frustrating man I know." She stood up and quickly walked back to her room. Hans followed, not so much to chase after her as to make sure she made it back to her room okay.

He went into his room, and even though the rooms were well insulated, he could hear her tossing things around the room. Then he heard her door slam. Where was she going? He wondered. He looked at his watch; it was late. He knocked lightly on her adjoining door; there was no answer. Where could she be going at this hour? He waited for what felt like a long time, but was really only fifteen minutes, and didn't hear her return. He worried about her. Where did she go? Was she okay? He grabbed his key and went in search of her. He walked down to the lobby and saw only a few people wandering around, and then he walked into the indoor pool. She had mentioned something about swimming, but no one was using the pool. Then he saw three people in the whirlpool. He immediately recognized Heather, her red hair in a bun, as one of the people sitting in the whirlpool. He stopped, but before he could decide what to do, she saw him and said, "Hans, please come, I want you to meet this delightful couple."

Hans slowly walked over to the whirlpool. He saw Heather sitting on one side of the large whirlpool and a couple that looked to be in their fifties sitting on the other side.

Heather said, "Hans, this is Hannah and Fritz Kopf. They are from Munich. Luckily for me they speak English."

Hannah said, "We came down to sit in the whirlpool, but found it occupied. Heather graciously invited us to join her. Then when we found out she was from San Francisco. Well, we love San Francisco, and within a few minutes it felt like we've know each other for years. Hans, your wife is such a delight."

Heather said, "Hans is not my husband."

"Oh, my mistake. We saw the two of you at dinner and just assumed."

"So where are you from, Hans?" Asked Fritz.

"Klingenmünster, a small village just east of here."

"I've got to know how the two of you met," said Hannah.

"Hans' nephew works at my firm in San Francisco," said Heather. "And when I decided to take a sabbatical to study the architecture of castles of this region, Hans' nephew suggested that I talk to his uncle about a guide. Well, after we talked, Hans agreed to be my guide."

"Well, Hans, we should all be fortunate enough to have such an insightful nephew. The two of you are so obviously in love. Who would have imagined?"

Hans stammered and said, "Yes, fortunate."

Fritz said, "Hans, forgive my wife, she is a hopeless romantic."

"Well, I think I am quite relaxed now," said Heather. "I will leave you two romantics to yourselves. Hans, will you hand me my robe, it's on the chair over there."

Hans went to get her robe, picked it up and turned back around to see her getting out of the whirlpool. The steam was rising from her nude body and the water glistening off it. His hands were shaking as he held her robe open so she could easily put it on. Then he wrapped it around her shoulders. She tied the belt and put on a pair of shower sandals. She turned back to the whirlpool and said, "*Gute Nacht*, Hannah and Fritz."

"*Gute Nacht*, Heather and Hans."

As they walked out of the whirlpool area Hans could feel the hot flush in his face and emotions rising in him. He had so many emotions running through him that were mixed. He felt anger that she went out to the whirlpool by herself so late at night, jealousy that she so willingly walked out of that whirlpool in front of that other couple, awkwardness that everyone assumed they were a couple in love, but most of all he felt desire, a desire that was hard to resist, and she was doing everything in her power, short of making the first move, to drive him crazy.

Neither one of them said a word as they walked down the hall to their rooms. As Heather reached into her pocket to retrieve the room key, she said, "Hans, it is sad that you are the only one who doesn't see it." She opened the door, walked in and closed the door behind her.

Hans waited in the hall for a moment; his hand stopped millimeters short of knocking on her door, but then he decided to go to his room. He did not sleep well; there were so many thoughts running through his mind. He placed his hand on the wall as if he could touch Heather, and wondered if she was sleeping.

CHAPTER SIXTEEN
ALTDAHN

He tossed and turned, and when sleep finally came, it was interrupted too soon by the sound of the telephone ringing. He picked up the receiver and heard Heather say, "Your facial appointment is in forty minutes. I assume you want to shower and grab breakfast before your appointment."

"Heather, where are you?"

"I am just starting my facial now. , I have to go."

The tone of her voice was not what he had grown to know; it had a brisk, business-like tone. It almost sounded like she was mad at him. What reason would she have to be mad at him, he wondered. If anything, I should be mad at her. He was a bit irritated. I wonder if that is her true nature when she doesn't get her way. He remembered how she went to the castle *Bewartstein* when he had asked her to wait. He was not accustomed to having someone take charge and do things without first consulting with him.

Hans was tempted to skip the appointment altogether, but that would be inconsiderate and rude. He must not let his irritation show and allow her actions to dictate his. He quickly showered and went down to the dining area for breakfast. He had his usual continental breakfast - two *Brötchen*, butter, jelly, a boiled egg, and coffee.

Hans viewed the beautiful surroundings and wondered if this was the type of life Heather was accustomed to. She was after all an important partner in a major firm, yet she seemed so at ease hiking in the mountains, riding bikes, and staying at the pensions. She confused him at every turn. He looked at his watch and realized it was time for his appointment. He followed the signs to the salon. As he passed the reception he saw Heather talking with the receptionist. When the receptionist looked up, Heather turned and saw him. She said, "Good day, Hans. You are just in time."

There was no doubt about it; the tone in her voice was distant.

He said, "Good morning, Heather. I trust you slept well?"

She replied, "Not at all."

He replied politely, "I am sorry to hear that you didn't sleep well. We can postpone our trip to the castle if you are too tired."

"No, that is the reason we came here. I'll be waiting until you are done, then we can go to the castle, if that works for you."

Until that very moment, Hans had often wondered how Heather had been so successful in a world dominated by men. To him she had always had this softness about her that appreciated art and beauty, but to take those ideas of art and beauty and turn them into reality took a different type of person, someone who could stand toe to toe with contractors, someone who was all business, someone like the Heather he saw today. But with this attitude, would she be a suitable partner? Why am I even thinking like this? He wondered.

He kept his appointment. It was an interesting procedure - the steam wrap, the scrubs, and the lotions all were pleasant, but he was not able to relax. When he was done, he thanked and tipped the lady and saw Heather waiting in the reception area.

She said, "I rented two bikes; I thought we could bike up."

Hans realized that she was indeed making all the decisions now. He wasn't sure he liked this new Heather. They rode single file through the streets, and didn't stop until they reached a car park area where they secured their bikes. From there it was a short climb to the castles.

The five sandstone cliffs spread out in front of them, causing Heather to quicken her pace. They went directly to the main part of the castle, climbing up stairs carved out of red sandstone that showed the wear of many years. Heather marched ahead as if on a mission. She pulled out her maps and sketches and quickly determined where she would focus her search and went straight towards the northernmost areas that appeared to have been residential. Instead of being a guide, Hans felt like an observer as he watched this woman doing a methodical investigation.

They moved from area to area carefully inspecting the mortar under any ledge that could have possibly been used as a window seat. It was interesting to note the water drainage system carved into the rock as channels. There were ancient carvings in the sandstone in the various cells/rooms. There were numerous cisterns for water collection. It was obvious that the architecture fascinated Heather. She would stop every now and then and just gaze as if studying the methods used to build the castle. The problem with the investigation was that sections of the castle had been destroyed and others suffered decay. Even so, they could see the various terraces, the weapons rooms, guard quarters hewn out of the rock. They went into the museum and saw pieces of armor and various models of the castle when it was in its prime. The outer face of the sandstone cliff showed the tiers of sandstone with varying colors depicting hundreds of thousands of years in formation.

Heather had the hotel staff pack a lunch for their journey, and now they ate sitting on a ledge overlooking the valley. The view was beautiful, and it was easy to imagine what it must have been like living here a long time ago. They hadn't spoken more than a dozen words with each other all morning, and Hans finally said, "Heather, you seem upset."

She faced him and replied, "You think?"

"Yes, I do. You appear to be upset. Are you?"

Heather grinned and then it became a smile. She said, "'You think?' is what kids say when they mean 'no kidding'."

Hans returned the smile. It was good to see her smile again. Then he said, "May I ask what has been bothering you?"

"To start with, this quest we're on. There's not much left of this castle," she said, showing her frustration. "How are we going to find a note here?"

"Yes, it might be difficult, but you know it did take us a while at the last castle until we found it." He paused and then said, "I sensed that you were upset prior to our arrival here."

"Now he's perceptive," She said shaking her head.

"What are you talking about?"

"Everyone in the whole place can tell how much I care for you. I mean, Hannah said we were obviously in love. I have been trying to let you know, eating the cake yesterday, the walk through the gardens arm and arm, staring up at the stars waiting for a kiss, but, no, you want to sit down on a bench. Hell, I even stood in front of you nude, twice. You, my ex-husband, and my doctors are the only ones who have seen me totally nude."

Hans said, "And Herr Kopf, from Munich."

She stood up from the rock wall she was sitting on and said, "Yeah, don't remind me. And he didn't turn and look, either. You know, they talk about the male ego being fragile. The female ego isn't armor plated, either. My husband slept with another woman. I like to blame my work for that, but what if it is just me? I am no longer twenty-five years old."

She turned her head. Hans got up, walked around so he could face her. He put his arms around her and kissed her passionately. His heart was beating wildly as Heather wrapped her arms around him. By the time the kiss ended, their hearts were beating as one. Heather's eyes were still closed as he broke from the kiss. He whispered, "Heather, I find you breathtaking. Resisting you has been the hardest thing I have done in a long time."

She smiled with her seductive smile and said, "Then stop resisting me." They kissed again.

"I can't believe I waited this long to kiss you like that."

Heather replied, "Me neither."

She took a step back and sat against the wall. Hans sat next to her and they began kissing. The moment their lips touched, they were catapulted into another time. Breaking from their embrace, the maiden says, "I cannot believe that it has been two long months since we have seen each other.

Her Champion replied, "I take it that was a goodbye kiss. Rumor abounds that your father is arranging a marriage between you and Sir William.

"I've told my mother that we have been together, as man and woman."

He stepped away and said, "Why would you do such a thing?"

"So that my mother will tell my father, and he will enter into negotiations with your family for my hand."

"Your father will never do that; it is not advantageous to him," he explained. "I am the youngest of many sons of poor nobility."

"If he does not, then I will run away with you." She said.

"Would you really?" he asked. "Give away all the fineries to live in our small castle, with my brothers and their families?"

"But you are so skilled with the sword and the lance, a champion at every game. You wear the finest of silk," she offered.

"I am the youngest brother. I learned to fight at a young age. I fight for prize money, sell off the trophies of silver and gold, make wagers on the side. I have fair ladies buy me gifts of fine clothing. You would best be suited to marry Sir William."

With tears welling up in her eyes, she whispered, "But I gave myself to you, I love you and only you." She kissed him deeply.

She was breaking his will; he loved her even though he knew it was wrong. He whispered, "I love you, too."

"I would rather die than marry Sir William!" she exclaimed. She stood up on the wall.

"No, please get down from there." He grabbed her, and pulled her to him. "Please don't, I love you too much."

She said, "Enough to keep me from marrying Sir William? Do you love me enough to take me away?"

He looked at her. Yes, he did love her more than he cared to admit, and responded, "Yes, yes, I love you that much. I cannot promise you fineries."

She whispered, "All I need, all I want, is your love. I'll leave the hook unlatched."

He was besotted, "I will be there, be packed and ready to go, as we must make a speedy exit. Your father and Sir William will be none too pleased."

She kissed him again and said, "I must take my leave. Until tonight, my love."

"Until tonight," he whispered.

Heather and Hans broke from their kiss. She looked at him and he nodded his head. Heather smiled, "I told you true love would prevail."

He kissed her quickly and said, "Maybe you are right, my dear. It seems to be with us."

She jumped down from her perch on the stonewall overlooking the valley and forest below, and she said with a smile, "I am crazy about you Hans Hess, and tonight I want to show you how much you mean to me. Now let's find ourselves a note."

Her statement took him back. Tonight, he thought. There was part of him that wanted to be with her now, here, and in every way, and there was part of him that was apprehensive about tonight.

They continued to search the chambers on the northeast side of the castle. It had the right angle that she had calculated. They searched hand in hand. Hans could not have been happier, and Heather was happy and excited. Even their lack of results couldn't sway their positive mood. The sun began to go down. Hans said, "You know, we have two more days to find the note. We can come back tomorrow. I was thinking about sitting in the whirlpool for a while, or perhaps strolling in the garden."

"You know, Hans, you are right. We can come back tomorrow."

Hans bent down to tie his shoe, before taking the long hike down the hill to where they parked the bikes. As he was squatted down, he saw some loose broken stones that had most likely fallen from the upper level. The two halves were held together by mortar, and in the mortar he saw a piece of tightly rolled paper. He could hardly contain the delight he felt when he said, "Or maybe we can just spend the next couple of days in each other's arms." He looked up at Heather.

"I like the sound of that idea, but we do need to think of the quest and the notes. We know our couple was here. There is a note here somewhere."

Hans picked up the two stones held together and said, "I guess you are right, we can't spend the next two days in each other's arms until we find that pesky little note, now can we?" The stones broke apart from the mortar and the note fell into his hand. He smiled and said, "How fortunate is that?"

Heather did a small dance. "I can't believe you found it in that fallen stone."

Hans slipped the note in his pocket.

"Let's read it," said Heather.

"No, we'll read it when we get back to Klingenmünster. The next two days are just for us."

Hans took her in his arms and they kissed passionately.

CHAPTER SEVENTEEN

THE NIGHT

The hike down to the park area and the bike ride back to the resort seemed to take forever. The sun had already set as they rode into the resort. Heather could not wait to get Hans to herself behind closed doors. She was throwing all caution to the wind, and it felt so right.

They returned too late for *Kaffee und Kuchen* and it was already dark when they returned the bikes. Hans said, "Why don't we shower and dress for dinner? Let's have an early dinner, take a walk through the garden and retire early."

Heather smiled and said, "I think that's a wonderful plan."

They returned to their rooms. As soon as Heather walked into her room she already missed Hans. She opened the door adjoining the two rooms on her side and knocked on it. Hans opened his door and whispered, "I was just getting ready to knock."

They kissed in the doorway. Heather could feel the response in Hans, and the way he made her feel caused her to be weak at the knees. His hand moved slowly to the front of her shirt. Then he pulled back and said, "No, I want tonight to be perfect."

She whispered, "Me, too."

They both took their showers; he had a towel wrapped around his waist and she had one wrapped around her body. She said, "You know, I don't know if leaving the doors open is such a good idea. That is if we want tonight to be perfect."

"You may have a point there," he said smiling. "Yes, we'll close them, at least until we're dressed." He closed his door, and she closed hers.

She combed through her curly red hair and let it dry naturally. She put on her slip and pulled out her red silk dress. It had some of the same lines as the blue dress, but the neckline was square rather than a plunging halter. She put on her make up, and was just about to put her hair up in a bun when she heard a knock at her adjoining door. She stood up and answered the door. Hans had his slacks and shirt on with his tie hanging around his unbuttoned shirt. He smiled and said, "Is this dressed enough?"

She responded, "As long as this is."

She sat down at the vanity table, and started to pull her hair up into a bun. He walked up behind her and said, "Keep it down tonight, I like it down."

"As you wish, my dear."

She slipped on the red silk dress and he smiled his approval. She helped him button his shirt and tie his tie, and then they were ready.

They rushed through dinner, although they were both hungry from their trip to the castle. Heather knew there were other reasons.

"Are you ready for a stroll through the gardens?" asked Hans.

Heather didn't answer, but rose from her seat with a grin on her face. Hans took her arm and led her to the exit and out into the garden. They continued walking until they reached that same bench they had occupied the night before. They stopped and took her into his arms and kissed her. He whispered, "I should have done that last night." Heather liked the feel of his hand moving down her silk dress; she could feel his excitement grow as their bodies pressed hard against one another. She moaned as they kissed.

"Perhaps we should go upstairs," she said.

"Yes, I think that is a very good idea."

They walked up from the garden to their rooms and he said, "Whose room?"

She smiled, "Your choice."

"Your room, then. It smells like your perfume."

He opened the door to her room and there was a sudden sense of urgency. They kissed as they rushed to get out of their clothes. Hans gently explored her body with this hands first and then his mouth, kissing her lips, her neck, and then one nipple and then the other.

Heather explored Hans with her fingertips, running her hands from his lips down his neck, slowly moving down, playing and teasing his nipples, and then further down, as she felt him throbbing from her touch, his hardness pressing against her. The second she felt him throbbing she wanted him in her.

They fell into her bed, and the kissing and exploring started once again, lying side by side. They looked into each other's eyes as they explored each other's bodies with their hands. His hands had moved further down between her legs; he moaned as he felt her wetness. She caressed him, feeling his throbbing want in, but his fingers worked their magic until she couldn't take it any more, her hips rising up, and begging him to be one with her.

He climbed on top of her and whispered, "I want you now." And as she felt him enter her, she moaned, and wrapped her legs around him. They moved in unison, their bodies became one, their hearts beating in rhythm, and he deep inside her. The level of pleasure was increasing with each thrust; she knew as they made love they were meant to be together. She felt his pace quicken. She held him tighter and then she heard him moan and felt the release. It felt so good to have him be part of her.

They fell asleep in each other's arms, locked together.

Hans awoke early, and for a moment didn't know where he was. Then he felt Heather's body still tight against him and he realized that it was not a dream, they had actually made love. Ever since their trip to *Bewartstein*, he had recurring dreams of making love to her, but had felt it was a dream that would never be fulfilled. Now here he was lying next to her. She looked so peaceful and so voluptuous. Just the thought started a rise in him, but he didn't want to awaken her. As he lay there, he felt her hand move to his stomach. She didn't open her eyes, but he sensed that she was awake. She slowly moved her hand downward, causing his member to rise as she placed her hand around it. She opened her eyes with a smile on her face as he placed his hand between her legs. She was already moist, and, without any words, they came together. Their lovemaking was unhurried, as he wanted to savor this feeling that had been so long absent from his life. She responded to him in every way. It felt so natural. It was so difficult to restrain the impending climax, and having reached a high point twice, the third time couldn't be withheld and they both climaxed together.

"Hans, what a wonderful way to wake up. I don't ever want it to change. It feels so right, don't you think?"

"Heather, my dear, you are very precious to me. I would want nothing more than to be together with you always. But I do think we need to take it a bit slow and think it all through, don't you?"

"I have thrown caution to the winds. I came over here on an impulse and things just happened as though it were fate. Those notes we found that caused us to go back in time to experience a love that has become real with us. How can we possibly ignore that?"

"I feel that, too. But there is something left unsolved. We haven't found all the notes and haven't learned the fate of those two lovers. What if something tragic occurred that would also affect us? Have you wondered about that?"

"I thought about that early on, but to be truthful, I didn't want to consider it since I was falling in love with you and wanted you. I chose to ignore that aspect of it. Was I foolish to do that?"

"I suppose when someone is in love, trying to be sensible is difficult. I must admit that I fell in love with you some time ago and have repressed my feelings on several accounts. The first you already know: the fact that I'm still married. The second is our age difference, and that can't be changed. The third is that you have a profession and a career, while I'm already retired. Our lives in that respect don't seem to mesh. I couldn't expect you to give up your career and I don't plan on moving back to the States."

"It does sound complicated, I must admit. But, Hans, if we love each other, couldn't we work things out? It would mean some compromise on both our parts, but we would be together. What I feel for you is more important than my career."

Hans pulled her to him and just held her without comment. His thoughts were racing. He needed time to think. This was just moving too fast.

"Heather, my dear. Let us just enjoy the time we have together for now. Let's be fair to each other and see how things develop. We are adults and need to be rational and not be too impulsive, although I must admit that being impulsive has brought us together."

"Okay, Hans. You're right. There's no need to rush. In fact..." she hesitated and then with her mischievous smile said, "In fact, I like it when we do things slowly."

Hans smiled; she had a way of defusing a difficult conversation and at the same time arousing feelings with a disarming smile. He kissed her on her cheek and said, "You do have a way about you that could make a man want to be forever in your bed. However, I need to replenish my energy." He rolled over and started to get up.

Heather looked at the clock and said, "Oh, no, we have massage appointments in less than an hour. My, my how time flies when you're having fun."

She gave Hans that mischievous grin and quickly jumped out of bed and went into the shower. Hans considered joining her, but decided it might delay their appointment, so he went into his own room to shower. His mind kept bouncing from one thing to another. Could he have more with Heather? He loved her and she loved him. Was it that simple? No, life was much more complicated. But for today and for the moment, it was that simple.

At breakfast Hans asked, "Have you made any plans for after our massage?"

"No, Hans. I initially thought we would spend another day at the castle, but perhaps we could visit the shops in town, and then perhaps come back here for *Kaffee und Kuchen*."

He grinned and said, "That sounds wonderful."

They went to separate rooms for their massage and Hans welcomed it. Although in good physical condition, particularly for a man his age, last night and this morning he discovered that he was using muscles that he hadn't used in quite some time.

After their massage, Hans and Heather went down to the village. They strolled hand in hand through the various shops.

Heather was beaming; being in love seemed to agree with her. Her demeanor was so upbeat and personable, a vast improvement from the previous day when she was so annoyed with him. Watching her interact, trying to use the German he taught her with the shopkeepers, was pleasant. Afterwards they walked back to the hotel still holding hands. They enjoyed the afternoon *Kaffee und Kuchen*. After walking through the gardens, they retired to her room.

Like their entire day, their afternoon lovemaking was so natural and unhurried. Heather seemed to enjoy discovering ways to please and arouse Hans. Hans never had such a partner whose desire to please was equal to his own.

They showered together, and then dressed for dinner. They took their time enjoying the wine and the meal as they talked about the stores and people they met on their shopping venture. They walked around the grounds before retiring for the evening. Once back in their room Heather said, "I can't believe this will be our last night together before we return to Klingenmünster."

Hans had not even thought about their return, until Heather brought it up. However, it did raise many questions. Klingenmünster was a small village. People knew one another. He couldn't stay the night at her pension without rumors spreading, and he could not bring Heather to his house. It would not be right. Suddenly he realized that tonight would be the last time they could be together intimately for a while. As a result, their lovemaking had an added feeling of desire and longing.

CHAPTER EIGHTEEN
A TWITCH

The next morning Heather woke first and curled up in Hans' arm. She decided to cancel her final beauty treatment in order to spend more time with Hans. When it was time to leave, they did so reluctantly.

Their drive back to Klingenmünster, while beautiful, was somewhat bittersweet. Heather knew that open displays of affection would not bode well in Hans' small town. She wondered when they could be together again. Most likely their next trip to a castle, but which castle? She interrupted the quiet drive home and said, "Hans, we still haven't deciphered the note."

"I was thinking the same thing. Let's have dinner this evening. We can work on the note and plan our next trip."

Heather smiled, touched his hand resting on his lap and said, "I do look forward to our next castle outing." Then she slightly squeezed his hand and his upper leg.

He smiled, "I truly enjoy every minute I spend with you, Heather. I have grown very fond of you."

Heather touched his arm and said, "The feeling is mutual, Hans."

When they pulled up to the pension, Hans said, "I must take care of a few things."

Heather nodded and said, "I understand. I too need to take care of a few things. What time do you want to have dinner?"

"Can we say 7:30? Does that give you enough time?"

"7:30 sounds wonderful." She squeezed his hand once again and got out of the car. She went upstairs, unpacked her things, and plugged her cell phone into her computer; she had a feeling she needed to check her emails. As soon as she logged onto her system, she saw a flurry of emails informing her that the meeting with the client had been moved up a week and preparations were needed. She had a feeling something was going on. The shortened time frame meant she would have to be more involved in the conceptual design for the presentation. She didn't have time for this, not now, not with things going so well with Hans.

***

When Hans returned home, he quickly changed clothes and then went directly to the *Pfalzklinik* to see his wife. He was curious to see if there was any change in her condition. He also wanted to sit and talk with her. He wasn't sure what he would say about his love affair, but he felt the need to talk about it, a confession of some sort, to clear his conscience.

As he approached the entrance, he didn't see Gretchen standing at her usual post. He rang the bell and waited a few moments before the door was opened.

"Guten Tag, Herr Hess."

He answered the greeting and asked about Gretchen. He was told that she had taken a few days' vacation, but would be back in the morning. He proceeded to his wife's room and saw that the nurse was making notes on her clipboard. She looked up and said that she was just finishing her routine check and invited Hans in. Within a few minutes the nurse departed and he was alone.

He sat on the bed next to his wife, just looking at her. She appeared to have a bit of color in her face since he'd seen her last, but that could have been his imagination. She lay perfectly still, as usual, and he couldn't help but make comparisons. His wife was rather small compared to Heather and her hair was a dark brown while Heather's was a reddish-blonde. Yes, they were very different to look at and they also had very different personalities. Of course, it had been a long time since he had been able to communicate with his wife and there were things already beginning to fade from memory. He was convinced that his wife was lost to him both mentally and physically, although she still breathed. He was now prepared to make a new life for himself and would no longer wait for a miracle to happen. It just wasn't going to happen, he now believed.

As he entertained these thoughts, he took his wife's hand in his and stroked it. He ran his hand gently over her forehead and tried to remember when she had responded to his touch. The memories were so vague. The more time he spent with Heather, the more distant became the memories he had of his wife. His duty to his wife – a devotion that appeared to be futile – simply had to end. He must make the break both mentally and physically. He would make sure that she was always cared for and would be available if there was ever a need.

"My dear," he said. "The last time I talked with you, I told you that I had found a new friend and that I thought I was falling in love with her. Well, my dear, I have fallen in love with that person. Did I tell you her name was Heather?" He paused and continued to stroke her hand. With the back of his hand he stroked her cheek. Then he continued.

"I think you would have liked her if the two of you had ever met. You may have even become good friends. She is very strong willed – a bit too strong in some ways, but she does know what she wants and goes after it. I admire that quality. And my dear, she has told me that she loves me, too." He paused as he noticed a slight flicker in her eyelids. *Am I imagining that*? He wondered, but continued, "I don't know how to tell you this, but we made love and…" he felt a small twitch in her hand. "Yes, I did feel that," he exclaimed out loud. "Monica, can you hear me? Do you understand what I'm saying?"

All was quiet. He looked around to see if anyone else had heard him, but no one was there. *Besides, if someone heard me talk, they probably wouldn't understand what I was saying anyway since they don't understand English.* With that reassurance, he continued.

"My dear, making love after so long a time did bring back some memories of you. Of course, it wasn't the same, you are both quite different, but…" he stopped. Did he see a movement around her mouth? First the eyes, then the hand, and now the mouth? *Am I hallucinating? Perhaps my guilt is causing me to see things. But I must say what needs to be said. I cannot be fair to Heather until I have been released from my wife, at least in my thoughts.*

He sat silently for a few moments and then continued. "Can you possibly understand that I must take my leave of you? That I must get on with my life? That…" Her eyes flickered. His pulse quickened at this sign of life. *It is as though she can hear me and wants me to know it,* he thought. *Should I continue, or call the doctor? No, I can't call the doctor, what would I tell him? I couldn't tell him the truth about what I was saying, and unless he saw her make the same movements, he would think that I belong in one of their beds here as well.*

He leaned over, taking both hands in his. He massaged and squeezed them. "Can you hear me?" he asked. "Do you know who I am?"

He felt a light movement of her fingers as though she was trying to return the squeeze. He released one hand to caress her brow and moved his fingers gently over her eyes. There was eye movement and the lids opened ever so slightly. It was just a crack, but they did open. Now he wanted to call for help, but didn't want to miss any more signs. Instead, he felt he should talk some more, but what to say now was the question. Should he continue with what he was saying or talk about something else?

"My dear. You know that I have loved you dearly for many years." And then he realized what he just said. He said, *loved*, as in past tense. *Was it all over? She is still my wife as long as she breathes. And how could I not love her? Of course, it is not the same as with Heather. How could it be? They are completely different people with an entirely different outlook in life."*

Hans tried to remember the coma diagnosis that had been made for his wife. For the three states of responses such as eye, verbal and motor, it was written: "Does not Open Eyes. Makes no sounds. Makes no movements." With this diagnosis, there had been little, if any, hope of recovery. But now there was some movement and he had to do something.

Hans hurried to the nurse's station and asked to see the doctor. The doctor was summoned, and Hans briefly described the movements he had observed in his wife. The doctor proceeded at once to his wife's room and asked Hans to accompany him. The doctor made a careful examination, but noticed nothing. He then asked Hans what he was doing at the time. Hans explained that he was talking to her when he observed the movements.

"That's interesting," said the doctor. "Please talk with her. I'd like to observe."

Hans didn't know what to say. He certainly couldn't continue with the same conversation, so he simply talked about the weather and about his visits to some castles, but there was no response. The doctor then said, "Sometimes there is something that will cause a reaction. It can be an emotion that could trigger some response. Were you talking about anything that might have triggered some emotion in her?"

"I'm not sure, Doctor. I was saying things of a personal nature, but I was not aware that she could understand what I was saying."

"There is much we don't understand about disorders of this nature. There are varying degrees of people in a coma. With many there are eye movements, some make incomprehensible sounds, some will respond as if in pain, et cetera. The fact that there has been no response until now makes this especially interesting. I would like it if you would try to re-create the situation that caused a reaction in your wife, even though it was slight."

"You're asking me to reveal some very personal things, Doctor. I would like to try it again privately, and if it does re-create a response, then I'd be willing to say certain things in your presence, provided, of course, that it would be kept confidential. Is that acceptable?"

"Of course. As for it remaining confidential, that is understood. You have no reason to be concerned about that."

The doctor left and Hans tried talking to his wife. He didn't know how to re-start the conversation and the mood just wasn't the same. Although he repeated some of the things he said earlier, there was no reaction. He finally stopped, kissed his wife on the cheek, and left her room. He saw the doctor and explained that there had been no reaction. Perhaps he could try again another time. The doctor agreed and wished him a good day.

Hans returned home, but didn't want to talk with Heather just yet. He needed some time to let this pass. He would not mention this to Heather – at least not yet. He had to be sure that there was some hope before he would bring it up. He called the pension where Heather was staying and asked them to let her know that he had some pressing business and would not be able to make dinner. He would call on her tomorrow for lunch.

CHAPTER NINETEEN
THE NOTE FROM *ALTDAHN*

While waiting for dinner with Hans, Heather opened the files she had downloaded over the Internet, reviewing the conceptual design for the new client. The minute Heather saw the concept, she knew the senior partners had not been listening to the client. She had done the initial research on the project, called and talked to the client, and incorporated their ideas into her proposal. The senior partners had been so used to doing things their way that they had completely missed the critical features the client wanted in the design of their corporate facility.

Heather looked at her watch. It was five p.m., and she would be meeting Hans at seven p.m. for dinner. She quickly did the math and realized it was ten a.m. West Coast time, a perfect time to contact her client and get some feedback on the conceptual design before their presentation.

Heather called the offices and explained that she was on vacation in Europe when the news of their winning the project came. She told them how excited she was about the project; however, she had not been in the loop and just wanted to go over a few things. By the end of the conversation, Heather knew the senior partners had missed the boat. She looked at her watch. It was six p.m., and she had time for one more phone call to talk to the partners before dinner with Hans.

The conversation with the partners was not nearly as cordial as her conversation had been with the client. Heather had written the proposal, had talked to the client. This was her vision and her project. The senior partners understood her concerns, but at the same time pointed out that they did the best they could do given her absence. By seven p.m., Heather found herself committing to redoing the entire conceptual plan in just two weeks. She looked at her watch and excused herself from the conversation. She wanted to prepare for dinner with Hans.

She quickly dressed in a nice casual outfit, put her hair down, put on a light layer of lipstick, and her perfume. She walked downstairs where the clerk gave her the note from Hans. Heather read it and was obviously disappointed. She went upstairs and wondered what business Hans could have that could have taken him away. Perhaps he was having second thoughts about them being together, as he did after their first kiss. Maybe this was his way of ending their relationship. It suddenly occurred to her that she had no way to contact him. She realized she had made love to a Hans Hess, and she didn't know where he lived, nor did she even know his phone number. He had always just shown up. What if he decided not to show up anymore? Her mind was running wild with doubt and second-guessing. She loved Hans, but what kind of love was that, what kind of fool was she? She buried her head in her pillow.

When she looked up she saw the conceptual model on her computer screen. She realized there was nothing she could do about Hans at this very moment, but she could work on her conceptual design, and if it took her mind off of Hans, all the better.

Heather sat down at her computer and began working. There was much to do in a short amount of time, and it was going to be a challenging project. Heather rolled up her sleeves and began to work on the drawings.

Heather fought to keep her eyes open, just a couple more things she needed to complete. She looked at the finished conceptual model on the computer screen. It had everything the client wanted, with function and form and, best yet, if done right it could be completed within the client's budget. She smiled, and felt her stomach growl, and then looked at her watch, it was two a.m. She wouldn't be able to find anything to eat this time of night. She saved her work; she would look it over once in the morning before sending it off. She took a quick shower and retired for the night.

Heather awoke late the next morning, reviewed her work from the night before, making a few last minute changes along the way. She smiled at her product. She plugged her cellular phone into her computer and started sending the file. She heard a knock at her door. She looked at herself. She was not at all prepared for visitors, and perhaps if she didn't answer they would go away. Then she heard Hans' voice say, "Heather, are you all right?"

Heather looked at her watch. It was ten minutes after noon. She closed her eyes, Hans had mentioned having lunch, but he never set a time. She rushed to the door and said, "Oh. Hans, just a couple of minutes. I overslept."

She quickly dressed and verified that her file had been sent. She logged off and shut down her computer. She looked at herself in the mirror; it was obvious she had been up half the night from her wild curly locks of hair to the dark circles under her eyes. She grabbed a pair of sunglasses and walked out to where Hans was waiting. They started walking down the hall and Hans asked, "Are you okay?"

"Yes, why?"

"You are normally waiting down in the lobby when I arrive," he answered.

She stopped and stared at him. It was the wrong thing to say after canceling last night. "Yes, I am, and I was waiting for you last night when I got your note."

"Are you upset with me, Heather?"

She responded as she continued to walk down the hall, "No, I am upset with myself."

Whatever for?"

Heather stopped and responded coldly in a whisper, "For sleeping with a guy who breaks dates by leaving messages with the front desk." She turned and headed down the stairs to the lobby.

Hans followed saying, "I am sorry, Heather. I had business last night."

"Well, Hans, I am sorry I was running late, but I had business this morning. I would have called and left a message, but you haven't bothered to give me your phone number."

Hans hesitated, and then said, "Heather, can we start this conversation over again? You look lovely today, my dear. I am sorry I had to cancel on you last night. I have a wonderful lunch date planned as a way of making it up to you."

Heather sidled up to him and whispered, "That was a very good recovery, Hans." She wanted to kiss him, but not here, in the middle of the afternoon, in front of people who knew him.

Hans opened the door for her as usual before getting into the drivers seat.

As they began their drive out of town, Hans said, "Heather, I thought of you last night. You have been on my mind quite a bit lately."

"I thought of you as well, Hans."

"I was thinking we could go to a quiet little place in Annweiler.

"That sounds wonderful, Hans. Did you bring the note?"

"Yes, I have it. Let's wait until we are seated and have ordered before looking at it. Okay?"

"Of course. But I am anxious to know what it says."

It wasn't more than a fifteen-minute car ride before they pulled into a parking lot. Then they walked through a very interesting *Fussgängerzone* to a small restaurant. Once they were seated, Hans insisted that Heather order for herself. After their orders were taken, Heather said, "Can we please look at the note?"

Hans smiled and said, "You are like a young child during the holidays."

He unrolled the note and they sat side by side as he deciphered it, until finally the translation was completed.

"My Champion, I hope you find this note. I am being taken away, to where I don't know. My father told Sir William of our love. His only concern is that I am not carrying your child. He plans to keep me locked up until the fall when we will wed in Trifels. Take care, my love, and exercise caution around Sir Williams's men.

"He never got the note!" Heather exclaimed. "Oh, Hans, what if he came looking for her and she wasn't there? What if Sir William's men captured him? What if she was forced to marry Sir William?"

Hans didn't reply. The next castle on Heather's list was *Trifels*, and he was worried. Heather was getting ready to go there to search for a note that he knew she wouldn't find, since he had already found it. It was the note he had put away and kept secret from her. *Should I tell her and avoid the trip?* He wondered. No, he thought, going to Trifels would allow them to spend the night together, yet he was worried about her reaction.

When Heather looked at Hans much of the color seemed gone from his face, so she asked, "Hans, are you okay?"

"Yes, yes, my dear, I'm okay."

"Well, you don't look it."

"I am fine, just hungry," as their meal was being served.

While eating, Heather said, "Can you believe it? *Trifels* was on my list as the next castle. That confirms it. We will go there next."

Hans nodded and then added, "I have some ideas." He looked up from his food, "I would like to meet first thing tomorrow morning for breakfast, and then we could leave from there."

Heather said, somewhat disappointed, "Yes, that makes sense."

Then Hans whispered, "I would like to stay with you at your place tonight, but I know Herr and Frau Wagner at the pension, and then of course there are nosey neighbors at my place."

"I completely understand."

Hans said somewhat cautiously, "Can I assume that I only need to make reservations for one hotel room near *Trifels*?"

Heather smiled her seductive smile and said, "I wouldn't want it any other way, my dear."

Hans reached across the table and squeezed her hand, and then held his glass up and said, "To *Trifels*."

Heather lifted her glass, touched his and said, "To *Trifels*."

They walked around the town most of the afternoon enjoying the historical sights and had some coffee at an outside café. Afterwards, they had dinner and then drove back to Heather's pension.

"I really wish I could stay with you tonight."

"I do, too, but I understand."

That night Heather checked her email to see if there were any comments on what she sent out earlier in the morning. She had a couple of emails about her changes. She quickly responded to them, and then sat down to read about *Trifels*.

CHAPTER TWENTY
THE HIKE TO *TRIFELS*

The next morning Hans met Heather for breakfast at the pension. They were both enjoying coffee with their rolls and jam. Heather opened the book she had been reading on castles and said, "Hans, you're not going to believe what I just read about *Trifels*! Listen to this:

'Trifels is considered one of the most important castles of the Middle Ages. In 1081 it was mentioned for the first time in a legal document. From 1125 the imperial insignia, crown, scepter and sword, the highest symbols of the Holy Roman Empire *were kept there. They stayed at Trifels until the end of the 13th century. In 1195 the treasures of the Normans were added, which had fallen into the hands of the* Staufern, *when they conquered Sicily. At the end of the 13th century the decline of Trifels Castle begins. Belligerent damages, a lightning strike and its exploitation as a source of building materials accelerated the dilapidation of the castle. In the middle of the 19th century the situation changed, in 1937/38-reconstruction work started with the aim to make Trifels a "national consecration site". The construction work, which did not exactly follow historical guidelines, was interrupted and finished after the war.'*

"Can you believe that? And there's something else. It says that between 1192 and 1194 *Trifels* served as a prison for the English King Richard the Lionhearted, who was captured when he returned from the crusades. He's the one I remember from the story of Robin Hood. It is all so exciting. I'm sure we'll find the note there. I can't wait to go."

"Heather, let's hike there. It won't take us that long and it can be fun."

"Yes, sure. I'd like that. We always have interesting experiences when we hike, don't you think?"

"Yes, we do. Go get your things and I'll meet you in a half hour."

They started out with a fast pace. They both wanted to get to *Trifels* by noon and have lunch at the castle. It was a beautiful sunny day with a soft breeze that helped make the walking pleasant. Heather was in a jovial mood and found amusement in almost everything.

"Geesh, Hans. You're looking awfully tired. Didn't you get enough sleep last night, or were you dreaming about something foolish again?"

"If I was dreaming about anything it was about how I would have to carry you when you collapsed on the trail."

"Yeah, right. And you think you can run rings around me? Is that with or without your clothes on?"

"That depends on if I was carrying you with or without your clothes on," Hans said with a chuckle.

"Hans, did you ever streak when you were young?"

"No, and I always wondered what it would be like. Have you ever streaked?"

"No, and I thought it would be fun to do it, at least just once."

"Well, what are you waiting for? Why don't you streak? There's no one here except me and the deer, my dear."

"You think I wouldn't do it? You think I'd be chicken to try it?"

"Yes, I do. You are all talk. You...." He stopped when Heather stopped and dropped her backpack. She started unbuttoning her blouse and took it off. She sat down and began taking off her shoes.

"You're really going to do it?"

"Of course. Are you chicken or will you join me?"

Hans thought he'd go along with the joke. He wondered just how far she would go before she stopped stripping. He dropped his backpack and started taking off his shirt and then his shoes. He thought he'd take off whatever she took off until she finally stopped. When he looked back at Heather she had taken off her bra and had a huge grin on her face when she saw him blush.

"Come on, Hans. What's taking you so long?" she said as she started taking off her panties. He stood still when she bent down to remove her panties as it caused her lovely breasts to swing free. There was an immediate reaction in his groin. Without further thought, he removed his clothes as well and they both stood naked looking at each other. Then they both began to laugh as he advanced toward her.

She smiled and said, "We are supposed to be streaking, remember." Then she took off running in the other direction and he pursued her as they both kept laughing at their foolishness. She finally slowed down and let him catch up with her, and they fell together on the ground, laughing even more. It was wicked fun. Then they began kissing and their hands began fondling one another as their passion increased to frenzy. He mounted her immediately and their lust was rewarded with an unimaginable sensation as they came together in an explosion of fulfillment.

Just then they heard a noise. "Shhhhh," said Hans, "someone's coming."

They hid behind some brush and watched as an elderly couple came walking up the trail. When they reached the place where Hans and Heather had taken off their clothes, they stopped and began talking.

"What are they saying?" asked Heather.

"They can't understand why the clothes are laying there. They wondering if they should pick them up or just leave them," said Hans.

"Oh, my God! No! They can't take our clothes. What would we do?"

They both watched as the couple picked up and put down the articles of clothing. Then the woman said, "Do you think the people are around here somewhere? They certainly wouldn't let these fine clothes just lying here. And besides, there are two backpacks."

The man agreed with her and said that perhaps they should be on their way. He said, "I don't think the people will come to claim their clothes with us standing here." With that, they continued on their way.

"Whew!" said Heather. "I thought for a moment we'd be stranded here all naked. I can't imagine what we would have done."

Hans suddenly found the entire situation funny and began to laugh hilariously. Heather joined in since it was so funny. They hurried to their clothes and quickly dressed. Then they broke out laughing again.

"I can't believe we did what we did. But it was fun, don't you think, Heather?"

"Hans, it is a memory of a lifetime. I never imagined that I would ever do such a thing. And I certainly never imagined that you would do it, either."

"So you thought I was too much of a prude?"

"No, it is just so much out of character for you. At least that's what I thought."

"Heather, I have been out of character ever since I met you. You have changed my life. Do you know that? You make me feel so young. Doing this was the craziest thing I have ever done and I'm glad we did it. And the love making was also special, don't you think?"

"Oh, Hans. It was wonderful. I felt so free, so uninhibited. It's as though we were Adam and Eve romping through the Garden of Eden."

"Well. I don't think I'd go that far, unless, of course, you start offering me apples to eat," he grinned.

They continued on their way along the path, the *Kramer Pfad*, and it wasn't long before they could see the *Trifels* castle in the distance. It stood majestically on the peak of the hill and there were two other hills with structures of some sort.

"What are on those hills?" asked Heather.

"The name *Trifels* literally means three large rocks that were made into mountain fortresses. One was used as a mint. Of course, today they are simply ruins. The town below is Annweiler, where we had lunch yesterday, and where I have booked our room there."

Just below the castle they stopped to have lunch at a large restaurant that catered to visitors. After lunch it was a short climb to the castle, but the incline was steep. As they approached the entrance there were many steps to climb and different archways to pass through before entering the main compound. This time Heather focused her search in the residential rooms to the west. It was in the exact location where Hans had found the original note so many years ago. She had solved the mystery, but would she like the answer? No, he decided, he would not burst her bubble just yet. Tomorrow they could come back and look for the note, at which time he would present it to her.

Even though their search did not bring result, Heather's mood was happy and playful. Hans was enjoying himself tremendously, going through the motions of searching the castle with her. There was a youthful enjoyment about being together; they pretended to be inhabitants of the castle. They peeked into the small chapel and then went to the tower that also housed a small museum.

As the sun sank, Heather said, "It has not been a very fruitful day, but I have so enjoyed being with you, Hans. Will you have time to come back tomorrow and look?"

"Yes, yes, I had planned on it." Hans replied, and then added, "Speaking of plans, I have some plans for this evening."

She smiled and said, "Hans, you are incorrigible."

"And what was your mind thinking, my dear?" Heather blushed, and then Hans said, "I hate to disappoint you, but I wasn't thinking of that, at least not until after dinner. No, I have made plans for dinner, and I have selected a very nice and secluded pension."

"You always plan the most wonderful evenings. I can't wait."

They hiked down the mountain to Annweiler. The town as seen from above was spread out in the valley with a stream running directly through it. They walked through the town along the stream with water wheels turning, generating power. The quaint shops along the way gave cause to stop and inspect the wares. Finally, at the edge of town, they walked into a pension. Hans spoke briefly to the woman, asking for their room. Heather noticed the woman flirting a bit with Hans and she immediately felt jealous. I guess I am becoming rather possessive, she thought.

Hans had reserved a room with its own bathroom so that they could have privacy. After emptying their backpacks, they showered and dressed for dinner. It took much restraint to continue with their plans since they wanted each other so much; however, the anticipation for the night was heightened considerably.

Hans led Heather to a quiet little romantic restaurant not far from the pension. There was music playing and it was obvious Hans knew the owner. They talked for a few minutes, and then Hans asked that Heather to read the menu and order for them. She said she would order a traditional dish, so she selected *Bratwurst und Kraut* for Hans and *Hühnerbrustfilet* for herself. They ordered a Cabernet Sauvignon wine. Dinner was light hearted and fun. The owner of the restaurant came up to the table and said, "I am Karl. You know, Hans and I go back many years."

Heather replied, "Oh, really?"

The man said, "Yes, he was here when he was a young man in the army, and he has a voice, oh, such a voice, all the girls would swoon. Has he sung for you?

"Just once, some time ago."

"Then he must again."

Hans said, "No, Karl."

Heather said, "Yes, Hans."

The owner talked to the leader of the band, after which Hans was invited to come and sing. Hans realized he was not getting out of it, so he walked up to the microphone, turned to the orchestra and said, "The Rose."

He began singing the song in German. The first word, *Liebe* (Love) got her attention. At the end of the first verse, Hans switched to English. Heather followed the words closely and understood how love, being compared to the twists and turns of a river, was symbolic of the struggles of life. She was mesmerized by his voice and the words of the song. He sang as though his heart was afraid of breaking, but, as with cold winter snows, hope was not lost, knowing that in spring there was new life. When he ended the song, she knew that the significance of the rose would always remain with her. The thorns in her life were being diminished by the beauty and power of love.

The audience clapped, and tears were running down Heather's face. Hans walked back to the table. Heather stood, hugged and kissed him. Karl came to the table and said, "See what I mean, even after all these years he has not lost it. He has won the heart of the most beautiful woman here tonight."

Karl sat down for a few minutes and talked about some of Hans' youthful escapades and then excused himself to be with other customers.

They topped the dinner off with a Peach Schnapps. Then Hans took Heather by the hand, led her from the restaurant, and they strolled back to the pension. It felt so right walking arm and arm. The sun was setting casting a bright orange tinge over *Trifels*. Heather sensed something significant in that, but kept it to herself. When they got to their room, there was no heated rush to passion as with their first time together or the frolicking playfulness earlier in the day. Tonight, it was sensual. They slowly undressed each other at the foot of the bed. They kissed passionately as they lightly ran their hands down each other's bodies, memorizing every curve. Heather kissed his neck, and then moved down to his chest, slowly encircling his nipples with her tongue. He felt his passion rising as her kisses moved down his chest towards his waist, and then she sat on the foot of the bed, facing him. She looked up, as if asking permission. Just the thought of her desire to please him in such a way was almost more than he could bear. He closed his eyes and nodded.

He felt her tongue and mouth work their magic, but she stopped short of bringing complete fulfillment, and whispered, "Not yet, my love."

She lay back on the bed, and he lay down beside her. Once again their hands slowly explored each other's bodies. He found the spot between her legs and she responded in such a passionate way. She whispered, "I want you to be one with me, Hans." As he entered her he heard her whisper, just audible, "I love you, Hans."

They took it very slowly, wanting it to last forever. Finally, after stopping short more times than either one of them could recall, they gave into their passion as they climaxed together. She curled up in his arms, her eyes closed, and her breathing became shallow as if asleep. He whispered just above audible range, "I love you, too, Heather." He thought he saw her smile ever so slightly.

***

The next morning, they woke in each other's arms and just held each other until they both knew it was time to get up and about. They ate at the pension, walked hand in hand up to the castle. Heather was playful and did not seem as focused on finding the note as she had been at previous castles or even yesterday.

Hans suggested they take a tour of the entire castle, including the famous chamber where they held Richard the Lionhearted and other high-ranking prisoners captive. Heather continued to be playful, poking him in the side, pinching his butt when no one was looking, and pecking him on the cheek at every opportunity. Hans enjoyed all the attention; it made him feel so young. She stepped into one of the locked chambers, and said, "Hans, you have captured my heart, take this key to my heart. It is yours." And she acted as if she were giving him a key.

Hans took the pretend key from her hand. The minute their hands touched against the stone wall of the dungeon, they were catapulted back in time. *She said, "Sir William, why do you bring me to such a hideous place on the eve before our wedding."*

Sir William said, "Soon you will be ruling. You must learn the duties, good and bad, of leadership. We found this spy lurking about. My men caught him before he made it to your chambers."

He brought the torch light close and when she saw the beat up face of her Champion, she gasped.

"So, my future wife, I must know, was this spy coming to rescue you at your beckoning or was his plan to harm you?"

Her Champion spat at her feet and said, "Death to Sir William and those who would bear his fruit." He glared at her.

Sir William smiled, "See, my dear, the price of leadership is high. There are always those who are willing to do just about anything to take what is yours."

She took Sir William's arm and headed up the stairs, "After our marriage you will rule by my side. You will be the most powerful woman in the region."

She walked up the stairs and said "Powerful enough to order an execution."

He laughed, "Yes, my dear."

She replied, "Powerful enough to grant clemency?"

"Yes, my dear, even that powerful," he said.

Heather and Hans removed their hands from the dungeon wall and stared at one another. Hans whispered, "He saved her life by saying he was sent to kill her, ensuring his own execution."

"And she married Sir William to grant him clemency."

They walked up the stairs and into the main courtyard in silence. Heather quickly headed up the residential chambers on the western side of the tower. Hans followed her. She frantically looked for the note, but without result. She turned to Hans and said, "There has to be a note, but what if there isn't? Does that mean she didn't pardon him? It can't end like this, Hans."

She turned and looked out the slit of the wedge-shaped window and whispered, "It has to be here." Hans walked up behind her, took the note he had been holding for over twenty years out of his pocket, and placed it on the windowsill next to her.

She stared at him and said, "Where did you find it?"

He said, "Right here under the window sill."

She was confused and then asked, "When did you find it? Yesterday?"

He shook his head, "No, I found it twenty-five years ago."

"You've had it all this time?" She said.

He nodded and replied, "Yes."

She held it in her hand and said, "You know what it says, don't you?"

Hans nodded again and said, "Yes."

She sat down on the bench next to the window and said, "You knew they would meet this tragic fate and you let me go hunting for these notes."

"I had no idea of their fate; I only knew what the note said."

She handed him the note and said, "Read it."

Hans unrolled the note and, without looking at it, said, *"I close these notes that tell a tale of a great love and sorrow. He was willing to give his life for my love, and I gave my love for his life. The notes have been hidden in the Castles where we danced, loved, and lost. They can only be found by those who are truly in love, soul mates, that will feel our love and loss as if it were their own, until someday our souls can be united as one. Whoever possesses this note must now seek the next note, and the chain cannot be broken without harm befalling the holder of these notes. The first note of our love can be found in the Castle Landeck."*

Heather just stared at him and said, "She gave her love for his life, and she married Sir William in order to grant her Champion clemency. You knew for over twenty-five years. You knew, and still you let me think it would end happily ever after."

She rushed up to him, wanting to lash out at him, but he grabbed her and held her tight. He whispered, "I didn't have a choice. Your life was at stake; the chain cannot be broken without harm befalling the holder of these notes. When you gave up the search, I almost lost you off the cliff, remember?"

She said, "You held the note for over twenty-five years, why didn't harm befall you?"

He said, "The notes can only be found by those truly in love, soul mates. I searched for the first note for years, then you came along, our hands touched, and you found the note. We are truly in love, soul mates."

Heather smiled, "Yes, we are." Then her face grew solemn, "So does that mean we will feel their loss as well? Is that our fate, Hans?"

Hans said, "Or it could be that someday our souls will be united as one."

Heather smiled. She thought for a moment, and then said, "That is a wonderful thought, Hans, but how will we know?"

"I don't know. From this point on we are both in the dark. I guess we will just have to take one day at time."

Hans and Heather spend the next week enjoying life as a couple. Heather told Hans that she would have to go back to the States to prepare and conduct the presentation. She showed Hans the work she was doing and he found her work fascinating. When it was time for Heather to leave, Hans took her to the airport. There were so many things they wanted to say to each other, but it seemed that everything they might say would only make the parting more difficult. Heather promised to return in two weeks, after her presentation. It was a sad farewell, not knowing what the future would bring. What they did know was that they were deeply in love and had become soul mates. Nothing was going to change that.

As Hans was returning from the airport with his mind still on Heather, his cellular phone rang, shaking him out of his reverie. He immediately recognized the number. It was the *Pfalzklinik*. He pulled off the road, answered the phone and heard an excited Gretchen say, "It is a miracle, Mr. Hess. Your wife, she is awake."

"Awake? What do you mean awake?" asked Hans.

"She has opened her eyes and seems to understand what is being said. I don't know if she has talked yet, but please hurry. It is so exciting."

"I'm on my way, but it will take at least another hour before I get there. Thanks for the call Gretchen. *Tschüs* (bye)."

Hans quickly got back on the Autobahn and moved onto the high-speed lane. His thoughts were racing. *What could this all mean? Was she going to get well? Was it just a temporary thing? Will she recognize me? Will she be able to talk to me?* His thoughts of Heather were pushed aside. There would be time enough to think about that.

He arrived at the *Klinik* and hurried to his wife's room, somewhat out of breath. The doctor and nurse were standing by the bedside and seemed to be holding a conversation. When they spied Hans, they both greeted him smiling.

"Herr Hess. Your wife has surprised all of us. Just several hours ago she opened her eyes and moved her arms. She then tried to talk. It was nothing we could understand, but we thought it best to notify you immediately. Please see for yourself."

Hans moved next to his wife and took her hand. She looked at him with both eyes open and a grin appeared on her face. Hans bent down and kissed her on her cheek and said, "Welcome back, Monica. Do you recognize me?"

She opened her mouth and tried to say something, but the words didn't come out. So Hans said, "Does that mean yes?" She responded with a slight squeeze of his hand and also by blinking her eyes.

"Is there anything I can get for you? Is there something you want?"

She didn't reply, but continued to smile.

The doctor said, "Herr Hess, I think you need to give it some time. Go slow and be patient. Perhaps it's best that you just do the talking and allow her to progress at her own pace." The doctor left and Hans sat by his wife talking about things in general. He described how things looked outside, how the flowers were blooming just now, and that the grapes were ripening in the vineyards. He continued talking until he noticed that she was growing tired and that her eyes were closing. When she fell asleep, he went home. His emotions were so mixed. Seemingly hundreds of questions were floating in his mind and he just couldn't sort things out. He opened a bottle of wine and sat alone in the dark. He thought about Heather and how much he loved her. He thought about his wife and the miracle that was happening. He wondered if she would recover fully, and if so, what he was to do. He couldn't leave her, he couldn't even consider that. But could he love her like he loved Heather? And what about Heather? What would he tell her? As the thoughts continued, he kept drinking until he dozed off to sleep.

He awoke with a start, wondering where he was. Then it all came flooding back to him. He was groggy, but managed to get up and make a strong cup of coffee. He decided to take breakfast at the hospital. He was anxious to see if there was any progress, any new developments with Monica.

He entered her room and noticed that her bed was elevated, allowing her to sit partially upright. Her eyes were open. He could see that her hair had been brushed, and her eyes told him that she recognized him. He went to her, taking her hands in his and sat next to her.

"Good morning, Monica. You are looking well this morning," he said with a smile. She returned the smile and moved her lips trying to form a word. She finally uttered the word, "good."

"That's fantastic!" said Hans. "Yes, it is good. Just take your time. There is no hurry."

There was not much change for two days, and then on the third day when he arrived, the doctor was in the room, as well as Gretchen. After his greeting, Monica said, "Hans, I had the most horrible dream. I dreamt that you left me for another woman."

Gretchen said, "Frau Hess, your husband has been the most devoted husband. He visited you nearly every day even after all these years.

His wife looked at Hans and said, "What does she mean by all these years?"

Hans glanced at the doctor, who nodded his head, and Hans said, "My dear, you have been asleep for a very long time, five years to be exact."

She exclaimed, "Five years! How could I be asleep for five years?"

The doctor said, "Technically, Frau Hess, you were in a coma."

"A coma? I was in a coma?" She whispered, as tears welled up in her eyes.

Hans' heart went out to her and he held her close. He whispered, "But you are back with us now, back with me now, and my prayers have been answered."

After the doctors finished their examination and everyone had left the room, his wife looked up and said, "Hans, who is Heather?"

Hans said, "What are you talking about?"

"While I was in a coma, I dreamed that you had told me you had fallen in love with another woman, a woman by the name of Heather. I tried so hard to wake up and beg you not to leave me. I could not go on without you. So, Hans, tell me who Heather is?"

Hans was speechless for a moment and then said softly, "Heather is someone who made me realize that I still had a life to live. She made me feel alive and gave my life some purpose."

Monica said nothing for a few moments. She looked inquiringly at Hans and then said, "Do you love her?"

Hans did not hesitate and replied, "Yes, I do. But I also love you. I never stopped loving you, but eventually came to understand that your condition would not change and believed that you may be lost to me. Can you understand that?"

Heather thought for a moment and then replied, "Five years is a long time. It is hard for me to comprehend what you must have gone through in that time and how lonely you must have felt. But I don't want to lose you. I love you and need you now more than ever."

"You're not going to lose me. For five years I prayed that you would come out of the coma and my prayers have now been answered. Perhaps it was Heather who helped spark your recovery."

"When you put it that way, I should feel grateful to her, but you must understand that I am naturally jealous of her affection for you. But how could she not love someone like you?"

Hans smiled. He took her hands in his and said, "Thank you for that compliment. Let's not talk any more about Heather. Let's talk about you and me. Okay?"

Monica smiled and said, "Yes. There is so much to look forward to now. I don't want to think of the past, only the future."

Hans kissed her on the cheek. Then he said, "It is so nice to have you back, my dear."

Hans met with the doctors who informed him that it would be several weeks until his wife regained enough strength to go home. Hans now debated when to tell Heather. He knew her presentation would be in a week. He decided to wait until after her presentation.

***

Heather arrived in San Francisco and hit the ground running, literally and figuratively. She rushed through customs, and then grabbed a taxi and went straight to the office. It was three o'clock in the afternoon and still several hours left before her business day was over, and there was a long list of things to do.

There was a nine-hour time difference between San Francisco and Germany. She quickly did the math and realized that it was midnight his time and simply too late to call and let him know she arrived safely. She would send him a quick email.

The minute she arrive at the office, she was besieged with people dropping by just to say, "Glad you're back." Karen had prioritized her emails, mail and "to-do" list. The number one item on her "to-do" list was a meeting with the senior partners at four o'clock.

Heather was getting settled behind her desk when Karen came into her office. "So, do you have any idea what this four o'clock meeting is all about?"

"Well," said Karen, "Scuttlebutt is that they missed you. Several of the key partners realized that you saved us big time by jumping in on this Syntec Corporate Headquarters project, while you were on leave. Your dedication and commitment to the firm was noticed by Kranshaw."

"Karen, I wrote that proposal, I met with the Syntec team, I couldn't let them go in the direction they were headed. By the way, thanks for the heads up. So you still haven't told me what this meeting is about."

"Well, the rumor is that they will be offering you a senior partner position if you take on Syntec. Nothing like going on leave for six weeks to make people realize how much they need you."

Heather leaned back in her chair. "Senior partner, they want to make me senior partner?"

"Yes, and I must say you deserve it." Karen said and then added, "Why aren't you jumping up and down and dancing around like a crazy woman? Oh, my, you met a man."

Heather stared at her assistant and best friend and said, "Is it that apparent?"

"The glow in your face and the fact that you don't seem to have any interest whatsoever in the fact that they are offering you senior partner. I want to know all the details," Karen said, smiling.

Heather's phone rang: saved by the bell! She wasn't sure if she was ready to talk about Hans to anyone just yet. She was almost afraid if she said anything she would jinx it. She answered the phone; it was the Syntec client, who was thrilled to catch her at the office. Karen took Heather's cue and left the room while Heather talked to her client. As the client talked, she sketched ideas that they wanted in their corporate headquarters. By the time Heather was done with the twenty-minute call, she was engrossed in the project and late for her meeting with the senior partners.

Heather handed Karen her sketch, asked her to scan it and send it out to the project team. Then she walked down the hall and into the boardroom and saw the group of senior partners, all male, all over fifty. She didn't belong in this group, and if she joined, what would it mean for her relationship with Hans? She walked into the room and without apologizing said, "I just got off the phone with the Syntec client. They are thrilled that Krenshaw, Martin and Wilson are on the project, and reiterated some of the key concepts they want to see in our design."

Thomas Krenshaw, the first name on the firm said, "You look well, Heather."

She said, "Thank you, Mr. Krenshaw."

Mr. Miller said, "You just got off the plane from Frankfurt and here you are touching base with the client. You are a real go-getter."

"I take my job seriously, Mr. Miller."

Mr. Krenshaw asked, "So did you enjoy yourself in Germany?"

Heather smiled and said, "Yes, I spent the entire time in the *Rheinpfalz* region of forests and wine country, touring castles. The architecture of that early period in history is so amazing."

Bob Ratchet said, "She is a chip off the old block. Your father couldn't go on vacation anywhere without studying architecture."

Mr. Krenshaw interrupted and said, "Your father was a hard working man with vision, and he was simply brilliant. We kept his name on the door for two reasons, one, out of respect for one of our best architects, and, two, in hopes that someday another Martin would rise to his level. Are you ready, Heather, to take the next step to senior partner?"

Thomas Krenshaw was her father's best friend. He treated her like a daughter, expecting more from her than any other staff, any associate, any junior partner, any partner. The jump to senior partner would be the biggest jump of all, with the greatest level of responsibility, greater demands on her time, involvement in the community and social events. She would be expected not only to bring big projects in, get them done on budget, but also uphold the corporate image. Her mind flashed to Hans. There was no way she could be a senior partner of one of the most conservative firms in the country and have an ongoing affair with a married man whose wife is in a coma. It was not something a senior partner could even contemplate.

She saw the looks of anticipation of the faces of the senior partners waiting for her obvious answer. But was it really that obvious? She had seen her father work himself into an early grave for the company. She knew the demands of the job, but most of all she thought of Hans.

Bob Ratchet said, "Heather, is someone else courting you?"

Heather thought her relationship with Hans was far more than courting, but that wasn't what Bob was talking about. Finally she found her voice and said, "Mr. Krenshaw, Mr. Ratchet, all of you, I am truly honored by this offer. It has me at a loss for words. It has always been my dream, and no, Mr. Ratchet, no other firms are courting me."

Thomas Krenshaw said, "I sense some hesitation in your voice, Heather. What is troubling you?"

She said, "I am jet-lagged and my mind is focused on the Syntec project." She smiled and said, "You know how to throw a girl a curve ball, don't you, Mr. Krenshaw?"

He smiled that fatherly smile of his. "You deserved it. And the way you set us straight on the Syntec project: that took guts! That's when we decided you need to be here in this room making decisions with us, not having to come back after the fact."

Heather smiled and said, "Do I have to give you an answer today?"

Thomas Krenshaw said, "It would be nice to go into the Syntec presentation saying this project will be headed up by our latest senior partner, Heather Martin."

Heather said, "I watched my dad do your job. I know how tough it is. Let's make it to the presentation and I'll give you my answer then."

Thomas Krenshaw walked over to her and said, "Poised and polished as always, Heather. You can give us an answer when you are ready to give us an answer, as long as it is the right answer."

The room laughed and Thomas Krenshaw said, "Heather, swing by my office in twenty minutes. I would like to talk to you, if it is okay with the rest of the senior partners?"

They all nodded. Heather took that as her cue to leave the room and made a quick exit. She walked back to her office and saw that it had been decorated while she was meeting with the partners. There were balloons and a big banner saying "Welcome back Senior Partner Martin".

Her entire team was waiting with champagne and a big cake. Heather looked around. How could she disappoint them? She said, "Thank you all. Now we need to get to work. We have a presentation to get ready in less than two weeks."

Cheers went up throughout the room. Heather spied Jordon Phillips, Hans' nephew, but by the time she was able to get across the room, he was gone. She looked at her watch and realized she had to meet with the Thomas Krenshaw in five minutes. She grabbed her sketch and rushed out of the room and went up to his corner office. His secretary Susan told her to go right on in.

She walked in feeling much like a schoolgirl being called to the principal's office. Thomas Krenshaw was looking out the window when she walked in, and without turning around said, "Have a seat, Heather."

Heather sat down in one of the two overstuffed leather chairs in front of his big mahogany desk. He slowly turned and said, "When your father died, I promised I would look after you. Not as a senior partner in the firm, but in a way a father looks after his daughter. There is something going on about this promotion and it is bothering you. Is it personal or professional? Several of our key partners think you are talking to some other firm."

Heather looked up at the man who sat at their Christmas dinner and attended her wedding, and said, "I told you before

I am not talking with any other firms. My hesitation is mostly personal."

Thomas said, "That's what I thought. Can I ask you what it is?"

Heather said, "Krenshaw, Wilson and Martin sets high standards for their senior partners. I am a divorced woman under 50."

He smiled and said, "Not sure you fit in the good-ole boy's club, huh?" Heather nodded. Then he said, "You are the breath of fresh air we need, someone who has the guts to remind us we are here for our clients."

She replied, "Yes, but there are all those social gatherings and I am a divorced woman."

He suddenly had a fierce look on his face, and said, "If it would have been up to me, you would be a widow right now, not paying that lazy, cheating SOB alimony."

Heather said, "And if I take this promotion, his lawyer will figure out how to get even more money."

He replied, "If that is the problem, we can defer your salary until the divorce is finalized."

Heather hesitated, then said, "That isn't the problem."

"Then tell me what the hell it is! Heather, you are like a daughter to me, and this is a chance of a lifetime!"

She replied, "And it will take up my entire life, to do the job right, and right now I am not ready to devote my entire life to work."

He stared at her and then his eyes lit up and he said, "You found someone, while you were on leave."

Heather smiled, "Yes, and the long distance relationship is going to be hard enough to maintain. It would be impossible with the demands of being a senior partner."

He looked at her inquisitively, "This must be some guy for you to be willing to give up the opportunity as senior partner."

"I am in love with him." She said.

He chuckled and said, "Now, you aren't going to run off and get married on me, are you?"

"Not likely. Marriage is for young kids having a family. We are mature people who don't need a piece of paper to say how we feel about each other."

Thomas Krenshaw replied, "I understand completely, and I can see why you feel that way after your divorce."

"Which, of course, goes back to yet another reason why I am hesitant about the senior partner position: the morals clause."

He said, "Well, once your divorce is finalized that shouldn't be an issue."

Heather didn't want to explain any further; it wasn't her marital status she was worried about. It was Hans' status. She now realized this was her best chance ever of getting Thomas Krenshaw to bend the rules for her, so she said, "Besides, I think it would be hard to be a senior partner and telecommute."

His voice raised and said, "Telecommute. No one in the firm telecommutes. That is completely out of the question for someone at your level."

She pulled out the sketch she was working on while talking to the Syntec client and handed it to her boss. He said, "What is this?"

She replied, "Your conceptual design for the Syntec corporate headquarters."

He unfolded it and stared at it in wonder, "Damn, you are even better than your dad."

"It has everything they want. I sketched while talking to them over the phone. I could jump on my computer, create it, scan it in and email to the team, get on teleconference, review documents. It is the 21st Century. I can do my job from over there. I won't be able to play office politics or climb the corporate ladder, but my job – this job – turning ideas into reality, I can do from over the pond."

He shook his head and said, "He must be something else."

Heather replied, "He is."

She stood up and said, "Well, I better get going."

He started to hand her the sketch and she said, "Keep it. I already scanned it in and the team is working on it."

***

Over the next two weeks Heather and her team worked diligently on the presentation. She talked briefly to Hans over the phone and traded emails back and forth. Hans seemed preoccupied, but then again so was Heather as she worked to get the presentation ready. She was also putting her affairs in order, hoping to facilitate the move as soon as possible. She inquired about a Visa to Germany and learned that she didn't need one. She worked on sub-letting her apartment until the lease was up, and was even looking at selling versus shipping her car to Germany.

On the day of the presentation Heather was nervous. She wanted this to go just right so that Thomas Krenshaw would allow her to telecommute and be with Hans. Krenshaw was the senior partner assigned to the project. They worked on their presentation and agreed not to talk about telecommuting until after the presentation.

The presentation was a complete success. As a matter of fact, not only were they thrilled with the concept for the corporate headquarters, but also they had five other major centers that they wanted Krenshaw, Wilson and Martin to design and build.

As Heather was driving to the airport, she called Hans. She said, "Hans, you would not believe it, they absolutely loved the concept. This is going to be some project. They have given us five more buildings to design and build."

Hans replied softly and said, "It sounds like it might take quite a bit of your time."

"I have already discussed telecommuting with my president. I think we can work something out. I want to come back to you as soon as possible. I miss you so."

Hans said, "Heather, don't give up the project you want for me."

"You mean more to me, Hans."

He cleared his throat and said, "I have some amazing news Heather."

With excitement in her voice, she said, "Please, Hans, tell me."

Hans cleared his throat again and said, "My wife woke up from her coma and she will be able to come home next week."

There was silence on the line and then after a very long pause, Heather said, "Oh, she's moving home. I take it she is moving home with you."

"Yes, Heather, she is. For years I prayed that she would wake up. My prayers were answered after I fell in love with you."

"And you have to take care of her." Heather said. She noticed a slight hesitation, and then a deep, regretful sigh before Hans responded.

"Yes, and you can't give up your career for me. I won't permit it." Hans said.

A million thoughts came rushing through Heather's mind. Hans would take care of his wife and he wouldn't have time for her. And even if he did, they couldn't be together, now that his wife was awake. Hans wouldn't cross the line, and neither would she. Life had thrown her yet another curve ball. Her heart was breaking in a thousand pieces. Finally she said, "Hans, we aren't the soul mates that were meant to be together, are we?"

Hans whispered, "Heather, soul mates we are. That can never change. It is just that we can't be together as one. There is so much I would like to say to you, but I can't find the words. You have changed my life. It is also possible that you triggered the circumstance, the response that caused my wife to return to consciousness."

Heather fought back the tears and said, "I am happy for her. She is a lucky woman. If I in some way helped her to be reunited with you, and if that will cause you happiness, then I can accept that."

Hans replied, "I can feel your pain. You will always be part of my life whether we ever see each other again or not. It is a sacrifice, but my love for you is eternal."

There was silence, then a muffled sigh before he heard the receiver click.

What was she going to do now? There was always work, but it could never replace what she had with Hans. Heather turned on the radio and the song "The Rose" came on, she sang along with the words thinking of the night at the restaurant outside of *Trifels*. She was angry and wanted to turn the radio off, but couldn't bring herself to do it.

That night Heather returned to her apartment, which was bare and already sub-leased. In two weeks she would have no place to live. She contemplated her options and felt a great emptiness. What good was finding true love only to lose it? What good was finding a soul mate only to lose him? But Hans had said they would always be soul mates. Her mind spun, her heart was broken, and sleep did not come easily.

The next morning Heather awoke to the harsh reality that her life had not changed: she still had a demanding job, and no one special in her life. The only difference was that she would have to find herself a place to live in two short weeks. She took BART to the office, and walked through the maze of cubicles. Then she saw it, the poster on Jordon Phillip's wall, of Hans near the *Landeck*. Her heart ached for him; she stopped and stared at it. Jordon Phillips looked up and said, "It is nice to see you back, Mrs. Wilson. I hope my Uncle Hans was of assistance as your guide through the castles?"

Heather just stared at the picture of Hans in the poster; finally understanding the sadness in his eyes and finally said, "Yes, he was quite helpful."

She walked into her office and told Karen to cancel all her plans for going abroad, that she would be staying after all and that she would need to find a real place, not some make-shift temporary apartment. She spent the entire morning meeting with the project team and then agreed to have lunch with Krenshaw. She told him she would be staying in town, but was not ready to be a senior partner.

When she returned from her meeting with Frank Krenshaw, she saw that Karen had left a stack of realtor listings on her desk. Heather thumbed through them, finding fault with nearly every one of them, and then at the very bottom of the stack, there was a picture of a dilapidated stone structure that looked much like a castle in Sonoma Valley with Karen's handwriting saying, every girl deserves to be a princess in her own castle. It was priced reasonably, for what it was, but much more than she wanted to pay. It had some acreage with a vineyard. It would be difficult to swing, but with her father's inheritance she might be able to do it. Heather called the agent and made arrangements to see the place the very next day.

As the realtor was showing her the property she said, "You know, I always thought this place had so much potential, and what a treasure. A German wine-growing family originally built this castle in the late 1800's from the Palatine region, or *die Pfalz,* as they say in Germany. They wanted to build a castle like one back home, I think they called it the…"

Heather didn't let her finish and said, "*Landeck.*"

The lady looked surprised and said, "Yes, how did you know?"

"I just returned from the region, where I spent quite a bit of time exploring the castles. I loved the original castle. I love all the castles from this period."

"What exactly do you do?"

"I am an architect."

"Then you are just the type of person who could appreciate this place. I was hoping that a university might have wanted to buy it and teach students about architecture and history."

CHAPTER TWENTY-TWO
THE ROSE

Twenty years later…

Dietrich Wilhelm walked up the stairs to the replica of *Burg Landeck* with his fellow students. As much as he hated to admit it, it was a good replica of the castle he had seen from afar in his entire childhood. This was going to be an easy class. Studying the architecture of the old castles, the first six weeks would be here at this replica initially built by an old German wine family in the late 1800's, and then restored with exacting detail by Dr. Martin herself, along with the help of hundreds of graduate students over the years. Then they would travel to Germany to take the knowledge they had learned to the actual castles of the *Pfalz* region.

The syllabus for the class stated that they would learn by living history. They walked into the main hall. He stared up at the large stones, and the tapestries that reminded him of the castles that he toured as a child; it was those castles that beckoned him to be an architect. He was impressed by the art and the tapestries; if they were replicas they were very good replicas. Then he saw her descending the staircase, in a flowing manner. She was tall, with waist length curly strawberry blond hair tied back in a loose braid with lace. She looked like a princess from the Middle Ages on the old art work, from her hair down to her shoes. She was dressed in period specific clothing, a royal blue full-length dress, with a simple jeweled belt loosely draped at her hip. Dietrich guessed she must have been somewhere between 18 and 25, with fine features and the most haunting blue eyes he had ever seen.

As she reached the curve of the stairs she said, "*Guten Tag.* (Good Day.) *Frauen, Ihre Zimmer erreichen Sie über die links liegenden Treppen.* (Women, you'll find your rooms up the left-hand stairway) *Männer, die Ihre Zimmer erreichen Sie über die rechts liegenden.* (Men, you'll find your rooms up the right-hand stairway.) Your clothing has been set out for you. Dr. Martin will receive you in the garden for *Kaffee und Kuchen* at four o'clock."

Tom whispered, "Hey, Dietrich, what is *Kaffee und Kuchen?*"

Dietrich whispered, "It is the German version of afternoon tea, the literal translation is 'coffee and cake'." Dietrich stared at the beautiful woman; her German dialect was flawless.

Dietrich found the room that he would be sharing with Tom. In it he saw tunics laid out on the beds, one forest green, the other royal blue, and immediately selected the royal blue, to match the beautiful hostess' gown. Tom grumbled about dressing up, but the minute Dietrich put on the tunic, it felt right.

Fifteen minutes before four o'clock, Dietrich headed down stairs where the beautiful young hostess was playing a harp in what appeared to be the music room. Dietrich recognized the tune, an old German tune that he had heard in church. She played it flawlessly. As she finished her tune, she looked up and saw him, their eyes met and then she looked back at her harp and played another tune. When the clock chimed four o'clock, she stood and walked into the hall, where the rest of the class had gathered. She walked through the crowd, as a sergeant would walk through a platoon, inspecting each soldier. She tilted several of the hats and straightened a couple of the women's belts. When she reached Dietrich, she stared at him as if searching for a flaw and then turning away when she couldn't find one. She led the group outside into a beautifully manicured rose garden.

Tables were set out with fine china, pastries and coffee. Dietrich caught his first glimpse of Dr. Martin, a handsome woman, who, he knew by her bio, was in her early 60's. She, too, wore period clothing, suitable for a matron.

She stood and said, "*Wilkommen. Darf Ich Ihnen Kaffee und Kuchen anbieten?* (Welcome. May I offer you some coffee and cake?) Over the next six weeks we will study the middle ages of the German gentile class by living their lives. A big part of our studies will be the architecture, but we will also touch on the history, culture, and other aspects of life in 12th Century Germany. Over the next six weeks we will begin to use more and more German, so you'd better brush up on your language skills. Then we will fly to Frankfurt and study the actual castles.

"I have tried to keep everything original here, importing many items to make the castle as close to authentic as possible. Speaking of as authentic as possible, you look wonderful. I trust you passed inspection by my daughter Rose." She smiled at her daughter and then said, "She is my most prized gift from Germany."

***

Hans made his way up the trail to *Burg Landeck*. It had become a daily ritual. He would arrive at the castle; touch the stone where he and Heather had first experienced the time warp, and then sit at a table in the open air when the weather was good. When the weather was inclement, he would sit inside at the *Stammtisch*. Being a regular patron had its advantages, one of which being an always-reserved table. He would reflect on that meeting with Heather on the drawbridge many years earlier, but yet it seemed only yesterday. Those memories kept him alive and vibrant. It gave him reason to keep coming here, and, in the process, gave him his daily exercise. It was now his pleasure to assist Heather with the instruction of her students. She had asked, and he had consented.

Today he was waiting for the arrival of her class of American students of architecture. This phase of their study gave them an authentic setting for their studies. During the course of years he had become familiar with much of the ancient architecture of the 12th century and could provide helpful insights to these students as their tour guide.

While he waited for the students to arrive, the memories came flooding back. Losing Heather had been heartbreaking. Getting his wife back had offset the pain of that loss. It had taken time to readjust with Monica. She did become more sensuous, he remembered. She was almost like a new person, not the prude she formerly had been. He tried not to make any comparison between Monica and Heather. They were both very different. Heather was vivacious whereas Monica was more subdued, yet always willing to experiment. Yes, he had to admit that they had a pleasant life together. They were careful to avoid any discussion about the child that might have been. He remembered when things began to change for her. She knew she was failing physically and didn't want to say anything, and when she did, it was too late. By the time she was diagnosed with cancer of the pancreas it was too far advanced to operate. After she was gone, he thought often about their failure to have a child. Now more than ever, he felt the need to have a child to care for and assist in some way. It was already two years since Monica's death and he was still coping with the loneliness.

His thoughts were interrupted when he spied the small bus arriving in the parking area. He watched as they alighted from the bus and then stood in a group. There were eight young students. A tall girl appeared to be the leader and was giving them instructions. Then they began their ascent to the castle. The walk of the girl leading the group seemed so familiar. The breeze would cause her to brush her hair back from her eyes and the sun reflected a reddish sheen on her head. His attention was now completely focused on this girl whose stature was remarkably tall and who walked like an athlete.

Hans shook his head. Was he dreaming? It was almost as though he was watching a re-run of an image he had seen years ago. "I suppose I'm just getting old," he said to himself. "Perhaps I'm beginning to hallucinate."

The group arrived and Hans rose from his seat to greet them.

"I am Hans Hess," he said extending his hand to the leader of the group. She extended her hand and looked at him inquisitively. Her blue eyes, the reddish-blond hair and her stature caused him to stare.

"I am Rose," she said. I am pleased to meet you, Herr Hess. We are excited to be here."

Rose looked at this old man as though she may have seen him before. His hair was completely gray. He stood upright, but supported himself with a cane. His blue eyes seemed to pierce her soul as if with an uncertain familiarity.

"Would you care for some refreshment, or do you wish to begin at once?" Hans asked.

"I think we shall begin and then we can take a break and have some refreshment," she replied.

Hans noticed immediately her take-charge attitude. He said, "Please follow me, and be careful of your step."

As they went from place to place, the students would comment on the similarity to the castle back home. At each stage of the tour, Hans would explain what they were seeing and how it related to that period of history. Rose provided additional information that she had learned concerning the architectural characteristics of the period. As she conducted her lectures, Hans continued to note the resemblance. He had mentally calculated her suspected age and it gave him reason for suspicion.

There was one young man among the group, Dietrich, who seemed knowledgeable and spoke fluent German. When Hans commented on his excellent use of the language, he smiled and said in German, "I grew up in Annweiler and have been studying at the University of California at Berkeley for the past four years. I decided to take Dr. Martin's class as a means of visiting my family. I must admit, I have learned more than I thought I would."

To hear the young man refer to Heather as Dr. Martin surprised Hans. He remembered when he was her teacher, her guide, and now she was teaching others. He could visualize Heather teaching; she always had that take charge way about her, much like the young lady Rose.

After their break, they continued the tour. When the tour was finished, Hans excused himself and went into the Café to be alone as the realization hit him. As he reflected on that time of his life a tear ran down his cheek. *And to give her the name of Rose. Could it be? Yes, that is something Heather would have done. To know the pain that Heather must have suffered keeping this to herself. To tell him about her pregnancy would have been too much for him to bear. She knew he had his responsibilities to care for Monica and therefore had decided to make the responsibility of raising a child completely her own. Sending Rose here was a gift of love. She knew I would recognize her and that is why she asked me to give this tour. Our memory of love is visibly alive.*

From his seat in the café he watched Rose walk through the archway with the other students. Then he heard a familiar voice behind him say, "She is a beautiful girl, don't you think?" Hans turned and there stood Heather. She too had aged. The gray streaks in her hair and the crow's feet by her eyes did not retract from her beauty. She appeared more slender, which made her appear even taller than she was.

Hans slowly stood up from the table. He refrained from using his cane and straightened his back to his full height. The lines in his face did not detract from the twinkle in his eyes. He extended his hand and she took it in hers. He placed his other hand over hers and she did the same. They stood looking into each other's eyes as though mesmerized. The many years of separation came together quickly as they were reunited in thought. There was so much Hans wanted to say, but he finally said, "She has your hair and height."

Heather responded, "And your eyes and musical talent."

"She is a remarkable young lady. She speaks fluent German, is knowledgeable of the architecture, and has that self-reliant spirit of her mother."

"Yet she has that kind disposition of her father. I often told her what a remarkable man her father is. I am happy you finally got to meet her. I have always thought of her as your gift of love to me, and I am glad I was finally able to share her with you, if just for a moment. She insisted on coming on this trip. I think it might have something to do with Dietrich, the tall blond headed young man from Germany."

They both saw it. Rose stopped to touch the wall with Dietrich standing next to her and his hand touched hers. Heather and Hans, still standing with clasped hands, could almost see the vision again through the eyes of Rose and

Dietrich. Rose was clearly a soul created out of love whose mate could possibly be found within magic of these castle walls. Heather whispered, "I wonder if they are the ones who will live happily ever after."

Hans smiled. He cupped her face in his hands, pulled her to him kissing her forehead and then lightly on the lips. He looked deeply into her eyes said, "I am sure of it."

"Come," said Heather. "I want you to meet your daughter."

About the Author

Abe F. March is an international business consultant and author, living near Landau, Germany with his wife Gisela. An active retiree, he enjoys hiking and exploring the local vineyards and can also be heard singing with a regional men's choir. Mr. March's career has taken him around the world to work in many areas from his birthplace in the USA to Canada, Europe and the Middle East.

His first book, *To Beirut and Back - An American in the Middle East* was published in 2006, and is a memoir of his adventures that took him to Lebanon in the 1970s. Mr. March grew up in York County, Pennsylvania on the family farm, and he served in the USAF from 1957-61. His business career got underway with the computing sciences division of IBM's service bureau where he held positions as manager of administration and operations analyst. He later joined an international cosmetic company where he rapidly achieved top distributor status and was promoted to vice president of sales development and product market management, an opportunity which took throughout the USA and into Canada, Greece and Germany.

With international experience and an entrepreneurial spirit, Mr. March started his own importing business headquartered in Beirut, Lebanon, for the distribution of cosmetics and toiletries to the Middle East markets. With an ease about him and a talent for developing business relationships, he also functioned as a locator of goods and services sought by Mid-Eastern clients before the civil war in Lebanon destroyed his successful business enterprise. Mr. March returned to the United States to start over, and was soon working on an international level once again. His subsequent work involved Swan Technologies, Inc., a personal computer manufacturer in West Germany, and back to the US to work with Stork NV, supporting a fleet of 1200 Fokker Aircraft. He officially retired in 2001.

OTHER BOOKS BY ABE F. MARCH

To Beirut and Back - An American in the Middle East
They Plotted Revenge Against America
(available from All Things That Matter Press)

OTHER BOOKS BY CONTRIBUTING AUTHOR
LYNN JETT

From The Finish Line to the Drill Line
Last Breath of Summer Magic (a romantic short story)

www.ingramcontent.com/pod-product-compliance
Lightning Source LLC
Chambersburg PA
CBHW031109260626
47172CB00001B/285